Daniel Wise

Summer Days on the Hudson

The story of a pleasure tour from Sandy Hook to the Saranac lakes, including

incidents of travel, legends, historical anecdotes, sketches of scenery, etc.

Daniel Wise

Summer Days on the Hudson
The story of a pleasure tour from Sandy Hook to the Saranac lakes, including incidents of travel, legends, historical anecdotes, sketches of scenery, etc.

ISBN/EAN: 9783337154745

Printed in Europe, USA, Canada, Australia, Japan

Cover: Foto ©Andreas Hilbeck / pixelio.de

More available books at **www.hansebooks.com**

MANHATTANVILLE, FROM CLAREMONT.

SUMMER DAYS ON THE HUDSON:

The Story of a Pleasure Tour

FROM SANDY HOOK TO THE SARANAC LAKES,

INCLUDING

Incidents of Travel, Legends, Historical Anecdotes, Sketches of Scenery, etc.

By DANIEL WISE, D.D.

ILLUSTRATED BY ONE HUNDRED AND NINE ENGRAVINGS.

NEW YORK:

NELSON & PHILLIPS.

CINCINNATI: HITCHCOCK & WALDEN.

1875.

PREFATORY NOTE.

IN the following work the writer has aimed to combine instruction with amusement. Its brief sketches of the unequaled scenery of the valley of our American Rhine, as the Hudson has not inaptly been named, and its outlines of the legends, traditions, historical and personal incidents, associated with its localities, are intended to direct the attention of young people to the only method by which traveling can be made a source of refined pleasure and intellectual improvement. Without such habits of observation and inquiry travel soon becomes the synonym of toil, and the fruitful mother of vexation and *ennui.* With them it is a text-book of information and a well-spring of delight—this is the lesson of our book. We trust our readers will find amusement enough in the story, which is but a slender frame-work for the lesson, to carry them pleasantly through its pages.

Our materials were derived from School-craft's great work on the Indians, Botta's " History of the Revolutionary War," Irving's " Life of Washington " and other writings, Hunt's " Letters on the Hudson," Mrs. Grant's " Memoirs of an American Lady," " New York in the Olden Time," sundry guide-books to the Hudson, Lossing's magnificently illus-trated and finely written work on " The Hud-son from the Wilderness to the Sea," and from personal observations.   Most of our illustrations are from Mr. Lossing's admirable pencil, and have previously appeared in his above-named work, to which we refer such of our readers as may desire a more complete description and a fuller illustration of this magnificent stream.   DANIEL WISE.

ENGLEWOOD, NEW JERSEY.

CONTENTS.

CHAPTER I.

ON AND UNDER THE PALISADES.

On the Piazza of the Mountain House—A Party of Six Described—
The View from the Mountain House—The Ancient Nobility of the
Hudson Valley—The Influence of the Concord Fight on those Noble
Families—Jennie Stuart Rebuked—The Legend of Spuyten Duyvel
Creek—A Boat Trip on the Hudson—Under the Palisades—The
Country Behind the Palisades—Legend of the Phantom Ship—Back

CHAPTER II.

YACHT EXCURSION TO SANDY HOOK.

On Board a Steam Yacht—Visit to Washington Heights—A Garden of Delights—The Defense of Fort Washington Described—
Jeffrey's Hook—Washington in Tears—A Daring Deed—Fame a
Capricious Mistress—Pleasant Valley—Wayne's Repulse at Bull's
Ferry—André's Satire—A Tragic Coincidence—Weehawken Dueling Ground—Burr and Hamilton—An Indian Legend—The Battery
—The Narrows—Fort Hamilton—Sandy Hook—A Hearty Lunch
and a Pleasant Ramble—Hendrick Hudson's Mistake—Origin of
the name Manhattan—The Return Trip—The Navy Yard—At the

CHAPTER III.

FROM THE MOUNTAIN HOUSE TO TARRYTOWN.

A Secret Discovered—The Song of the Frog, Okogis—A Sail to
Tarrytown Proposed—On the River—Yonkers and its Name—A

CHAPTER IV.

SUNNYSIDE.

CHAPTER V.

FROM SLEEPY HOLLOW TO ROCKLAND LAKE.

CHAPTER VI.

FROM TARRYTOWN TO STONY POINT.

CHAPTER VII.

THROUGH THE HIGHLANDS.

CHAPTER VIII.

AT WEST POINT.

CHAPTER IX.

FROM WEST POINT TO NEWBURGH.

CHAPTER X.

FROM NEWBURGH TO THE KATZBERGS.

CHAPTER XI.

AMONG THE KATZKILLS.

CHAPTER XII.

FROM THE KATZKILLS TO ALBANY.

CHAPTER XIII.

FROM TROY TO THE FALLS OF THE BATTENKILL.

CHAPTER XIV.

FROM THE BATTENKILL TO LAKE GEORGE.

CHAPTER XV.

FROM LAKE GEORGE TO THE PEAK OF TAHAWUS.

CHAPTER XVI.

FROM TAHAWUS TO THE END OF THE TOUR.

Illustrations.

SUMMER DAYS ON THE HUDSON.

CHAPTER I.

ON AND UNDER THE PALISADES.

IMAGINE a bright, bland morning in June. A
party of six is seated on the spacious piazza of
the Mountain House, which stands on the Palisades
of our noble Hudson, near the beautiful village of
Englewood. The seniors of this little coterie are
Colonel Charles Macintosh, a rich bachelor, on the
shady side of fifty, and his sister, Mrs. Ida Stuart,
a widow somewhat older. The colonel is a man of
commanding height, aspect, and manner. His air
is military. His oval face is well covered with
beard, mustache, and whiskers, all which, like his
hair, are iron-gray. His clear, dark eyes, though
restless and penetrating, have in them a softened
light, which proclaims the presence of a kindly
spirit, as does the smile which is constantly playing,
like rays of sunshine, from his thin, finely chiseled
lips. A distant view of the colonel might repel the
advances of a stranger. A nearer approach would

both command his respect and invite his confidence. Moreover, the colonel is a *Christian* gentleman.

Mrs. Stuart is unlike her brother in form and manner. She is short, stout, round as a dumpling, with no stateliness in her manner; but she has the same kindly expression beaming from her blue eyes and playing on her lips. In her prime she was a blonde, and was regarded as a beauty. Even now she is a matronly lady who attracts attention, and favorably impresses all who behold her.

The young ladies of the party are Edith and Jennie Stuart, the widow's pretty daughters. The former is small—a blonde—the reproduction of Mrs. Stuart as she was when of Edith's age, "sweet seventeen;" the latter, who is approaching sixteen, is somewhat tall, has dark hair and eyes, finely cut features, and is as lively and capricious as her sister is demure and steadfast.

Two lads, the sons of a dear deceased friend of the colonel, complete the six. They have been adopted by him, have taken his name, and call him father. They are about the same ages as the young misses, whom they call their cousins, are quite good looking, and are, like them, enjoying their summer vacation. The elder is named Arthur, the younger, Clarence.

Having thus introduced our party to the reader,

we invite him to listen awhile to their conversation. The colonel is just saying to his sister :—

"I never tire of this glorious view. Its extent is so great, its objects so numerous and varied, one always finds something, not observed before, to interest him. At our feet we have the noblest of rivers, not inaptly called by some the Rhine of America. To the south lies New York, with its steepled churches, and its outline marked by a narrow forest of masts. Sweeping along to the eastward is Long Island, dotted with countless pretty villages, and with the glittering waters of its noble Sound, whitened by many a sail, stretched at its feet. Between us and that fine body of water we have the wooded hills of Westchester, crowned with beautiful cottages and stately mansions, the homes of honest toil, thrifty enterprise, and cultivated tastes. Looking north-eastward we see Connecticut in the distance, and nearer to us we have our river bank, on which sits Yonkers, like a princess in some vast drawing-room. But for the green woods which crown these rude rocks we might see far to the north and west across the thrifty State of New Jersey. As it is, the hoary tops of the Ramapo hills look down upon us when we look to the west. Positively I never saw a more attractive view, even in Europe."

"And positively I never heard my uncle talk so eloquently," said Miss Jennie, looking archly at the colonel, and laughing.

"Jennie!" exclaimed her sister, looking very gravely, "how can you speak so to Uncle Charles?"

The colonel gave no attention to his nieces, but continued gazing in rapt attention on the magnificent landscape. His sister, after shaking her head reprovingly at the vivacious Jennie, remarked,

"Yes, the view is fine, incomparably so in some respects. I do not wonder that, in earlier times, many nobles from Holland, France, and England, divided yonder broad acres sloping back from this glorious river into great estates; nor that they sought to rule, like ancient barons, over the poorer emigrants from their native land."

"Nobles, mamma! Do you mean to say—do you believe, I mean—that noble men and titled ladies from Europe were ever settled along the banks of the Hudson?"

To this question, put by the merry-minded Jennie, Mrs. Stuart replied:—

"Certainly, my child. The De Lanceys, Kips, Van Burggs, Stuyvesants, Van Rensselaers, De Peysters, Phillipses, and many others, were people of rank in Europe. They became patroons, and ruled their tenants like barons on yonder lands. They

Courtly style of the Hudson River gentry.

lived in courtly style, dressed in gold-laced velvet coats, wore big wigs, ruffles, and wide sleeves. They carried rapiers, and were 'the gentry of the country, to whom the country, without a rebellious thought, took off its hat.' Their tenants gathered at times by hundreds and by thousands, like the ancient clansmen in Scotland at the call of their chiefs. They were people of real dignity, too. Joseph Bonaparte, who, in later times, like Louis Philippe, Lafayette, and other notables, visited the Livingston manor, once said to a daughter of this family, 'Your mother should have been a queen.' "

"What you say reminds me, aunt, of a stanza in a poem by Holmes," observed Arthur, who, by the way, was much given to reading. "Shall I repeat it?"

"By all means," replied Mrs. Stuart with an approving smile.

Arthur then recited the following lines, descriptive of the effect produced by a gentleman's turnout in the olden time :—

> "And all the midland counties through,
>   The plowman stopp'd to gaze,
> Where'er his chariot swept in view
>   Behind the shining bays,
> With mute obeisance, grave and slow
>   Repaid by bow polite—
> *For such the way, with high and low,*
>   *Till after Concord's fight."*

20   SUMMER DAYS ON THE HUDSON.

Effect of the Concord fight.   Jennie's anger.

"Ah! that Concord fight was a wonderful event!" exclaimed the colonel. "It began a new epoch in the world's history. But for that barons might still have lived in slothful pomp, and vassals toiled in hopeless poverty, all over yonder beautiful hills, and through large portions of this country."

"Then I wish that Concord fight had never taken place," replied Jennie, drawing herself up proudly. "I think it would be very nice to live in a baronial castle, with crowds of vassals to serve you and to do you reverence when you rode out on your palfrey, followed by a troop of gay young knights."

"Nice for whom, Cousin Jennie, the barons and their families, or the poor cringing vassals?" asked Clarence in a bantering tone.

Jennie's dark eyes flashed with resentful feeling as she retorted, in an offended tone,

"For the barons, of course, Mr. Macintosh! You don't suppose that I should have been a churl's daughter, do you?"

Poor Clarence, who was anxious to keep on good terms with his lively cousin, shrank before this outburst of girlish anger and pride, and looked appealingly to the colonel, who came to his relief by saying,

"Tut, tut, Miss Jennie. You might have been a vassal's daughter, and yet the superior of your mistress in every thing that constitutes true nobility. Remember, my dear, that a poor maiden adorned with Christian virtues is more noble than baroness or princess whose soul is corrupted by pride, vanity, and selfishness."

Jennie's eyes fell beneath this pointed rebuke. She pouted and moved uneasily in her chair, when . Arthur very good-naturedly came to her relief by touching the colonel's arm, pointing across the river to a small stream flowing beneath a railway bridge, and asking,

"Is that little stream the creek of which Irving speaks in his Diedrich Knickerbocker's famous History of New York, as the place where Anthony, the Dutch trumpeter, was carried down by the Evil One?"

"Yes, Arthur, that is the Spuyten Duyvel Creek. Suppose you give us the legend."

Arthur said he had Diedrich's famous history in his room and would read it, which he did, after getting the volume, as follows:—

"The wind was high, the elements were in an uproar, and no Charon could be found to ferry the adventurous sounder of brass across the water. For a short time he vapored like an impatient ghost upon the brink, and then, bethinking himself of the urgency of his errand, (which was to rouse the

people beyond the creek to arm and defend themselves against the English, who had come to de-
mand possession of the city and province of New

SPUYTEN DUYVEL CREEK.

Amsterdam,) he took a hearty embrace of his stone
bottle, swore most valorously that he would swim
across in spite of the devil, (*en spyt den duyvel,*)
and daringly plunged into the stream. Luckless
Anthony! Scarcely had he buffeted half way over

when he was observed to struggle violently, as if battling with the spirit of the waters. Instinctively he put his trumpet to his mouth, and giving a vehement blast, sank forever to the bottom! The clangor of his trumpet, like that of the ivory horn of the renowned paladin, Orlando, when expiring on the glorious field of Roncesvalles, rang far and wide through the country, alarming the neighbors round, who hurried in amazement to the spot. Here an old Dutch burgher, famed for his veracity, and who had been a witness of the fact, related to them the melancholy affair; with the fearful addition, [to which I am slow in giving belief,] that he saw the duyvel, in the shape of a huge moss-bunker, (a species of inferior fish,) seize the sturdy Anthony by the leg and drag him beneath the waves. Certain it is, the place, with the adjoining promontory which projects into the Hudson, has been called *Spyt den Duyvel* ever since."

" How funny!" exclaimed the vivacious Jennie, who had by this time recovered from the effects of her uncle's reproof.

" But it is not true," observed Edith gravely.

" Not wholly," replied the colonel. " It is possible that, when the English landed to attack the burghers of New Amsterdam, as New York was then named, a messenger, sent to alarm the colo-

24   SUMMER DAYS ON THE HUDSON.

Ghostly fears of the Dutch colonists.   A boat trip proposed.

nists, was drowned in an attempt to swim the creek. All beyond this is legendary, a mingling of much superstitious belief with a little fact. The old Dutch colonists were very much given to ghostly fears. Do you remember Washington Irving's story of Dolph Heyliger, Arthur?"

Arthur laughed, and replied that he had read it more than once, and was very much delighted with Dolph's adventures in the Haunted House and on the Hudson, especially with his success in winning the pretty Marie Vander Heyden for his bride. He hoped, he said laughingly, that he should be as fortunate when he himself should be old enough to win some fair maiden.

This last sentence was accompanied with a mischievous glance at Miss Jennie, who blushed, tittered, and said to her sister,

" How silly Cousin Arthur can talk when he tries, can't he, Edith ?"   .

But Edith's attention was diverted to Clarence, who was proposing a boat trip up the river for the younger members of the party.

" I should like it very much indeed," she said. Then turning to Jennie, who was pouting in her prettiest way over her sister's inattention to her question, she added,

" What do you say to that, Jennie ?"

" To what ? "

" To a row up the river."

" I should like it much if we only had some one to row whom we could trust."

As Jennie said this she cast a scornful glance on her cousins, on Arthur especially. But Clarence, unmindful of her scorn, insisted that he and Arthur were counted the best rowers in the freshman crew at their college, and were eminently worthy of being trusted with the safety of the young ladies, to whom, he said playfully, he would pledge his knightly honor that " they should be returned to their lady mother without a wrinkle."

" Without a *wrinkle !* " exclaimed Jennie, with flashing eyes, " what impudence ! One would imagine we were a couple of ancient maidens of uncertain age to hear him talk. I have a great mind not to stir a step with him."

Clarence explained his remark by saying that he only intended to pledge himself that no weird influence should lull the young ladies into a sleep like that which overtook the famous Rip Van Winkle higher up the river; but that they should be duly returned in two or three hours in all the beautiful freshness of their youth and beauty.

Jennie muttered something about " beautiful nonsense," but went with her sister for her straw flat

2

and parasol. A few minutes later the four were
seen descending the steep, romantic foot-path which
winds from near the "Mountain House" through
yawning ravines, past huge masses of trap-rock,
down to the steamboat dock, some four hundred
feet or more below. Here they hired a boat,
which the young men rowed up the river two
or three miles, keeping near the western shore so
as to gain a near view of those remarkable masses
of trap known as the Palisades of the Hudson
River.

"What horrid rocks those are!" exclaimed Jennie, as Arthur rowed close in shore where the range
reached to nearly its loftiest height; "they look as
if there might be a desert filled with wild beasts behind them."

Edith thought, that though they were rude and
wild there was a savage grandeur about them which
awed her spirit.

Arthur agreed with Edith, as indeed he generally
did in his opinions, though Jennie was his favorite.
Clarence sided with the latter, and said :—

"That remarkable ledge excites my wonder, not
my admiration. I try to fancy sometimes the wild
tumult of the hour in which this trap came burning
hot from beneath the sandstone, along a narrow
line not over a mile in width, and reaching all the

What Clarence wished.

UNDER THE PALISADES.

was a grand movement of old Mother Nature. O
that I had been here to see it!"

"You would have been alone in your glory, then,"
replied Arthur, "for this trap was upheaved before
our unfortunate father, Adam, saw the light."

"I wonder if there are any bears or wolves on the
top!" exclaimed Jennie, shuddering slightly as if
she fancied the possibility of being seized and carried off by some imaginary wild beast.

"Why Jennie, don't you know better?" asked
Edith in a half rebukeful tone. "Haven't we driv-
en to Tenafly, Cresskill, and Alpine, which lie right·
back of these mighty rocks?"

Jennie had forgotten this; and Edith proceeded
to express her admiration of the beautiful slope and
valley which lie in rare and quiet beauty behind the
Palisades.

Clarence was surprised, he said, that this valley
had been so long neglected by New Yorkers, especially in view of its remarkable healthfulness.
"Think of it!" he exclaimed. "There is Englewood township, with its four thousand inhabitants,
and only forty deaths in a year. One death to
one hundred and twenty-five people! Why, if the
whole valley is like· Englewood it is a perfect sani-
tarium, one of the healthiest places in the land."

Arthur suggested laughingly that if he didn't

know his brother to be as poor as Job's turkey, he should take him to be a speculator in real estate, with "lots" beautifully mapped out, and waiting for buyers at fancy prices. Then, resting on his oar, he pointed to a top-sail schooner which was sailing toward them, and said,

"I could easily fancy yonder vessel sailing so close to the bluff to be the Storm Ship which, according to the old Dutch colonists, once haunted this grand old river."

"Tell us about it, Arthur," pleaded Edith.

Arthur, whose head was a library of legends, gave the oars to his brother, who rowed slowly down the river while Arthur told the legend of the Storm Ship, as related by Irving in his veritable story of Dolph Heyliger. How she came across the ocean freighted with ghostly Dutchmen, wearing high-crowned hats with feathers. How she frightened the portly old mynheers of New Amsterdam. How the redoubtable old Captain Hans Van Pelt vainly sought to board her, how she sailed far up the river, no one knew whither, and how she appeared and disappeared at different times and various places, to the terror of the Dutch skippers and their crews, whose vessels sailed on these haunted waters. This weird story, the sleepy air, which seemed to be wooing the still, sunlit water to its embraces, and

the steady motion of the skiff so beguiled the fleet-
ing hours, that when the boat touched her landing-
place they were all surprised to find, on looking at
their watches, that the afternoon was fast wearing
away.

"We shall have barely time to get rested and
dress for dinner," said Jennie as she skipped across
the beach to the rustic foot-path leading up to the
"Mountain House."

CHAPTER II.

YACHT EXCURSION TO SANDY HOOK.

A DAY or two after their pleasant boat trip the young folks were greatly delighted by an invitation to go down the river to Sandy Hook in a small steam yacht owned by a friend of the colonel. This little craft, which was pronounced a "perfect little beauty" by the young ladies, found our joyous party on the wharf at eight o'clock, and after taking them on board, steamed away at once to Washington Heights, formerly Mount Washington.

The colonel, full of the military associations connected with this locality, requested the captain of the yacht to land them at a small wharf whence they could readily ascend the height.

" How beautiful!" exclaimed Edith as the party reached a point in the road from which a charming villa, standing upon the summit of a sloping, smoothly shaven lawn, came into view.

" It's perfectly splendid!" replied her lively sister.

" Just peep between those trees," said Clarence, pointing backward. " See those bold bluffs yonder! See, too, the face of old Father Hudson shimmer-

VIEW ON WASHINGTON HEIGHTS.

ing in the sunshine. Its ripples look like happy smiles."

"How poetical we are!" retorted Jennie, with a little sarcastic laugh.

" We can afford to be poetical," said the patriotic colonel. " Nature and art have combined to make this spot a garden of delights. Yet I cannot help sighing when I think that we are walking over the dust of heroes and patriots, and that the food which gives the roses and lilies of yonder pleasure grounds their richest tints comes, in part at least, from the remains of brave men whose blood was freely spilt in defense of liberty."

" O, uncle! I hope you don't mean to say that we are walking over dead men's bones!" cried Jennie, with an expression of horror which was partly affected and partly real.

" Perhaps not their *bones*, my dear, but their dust certainly. We are passing over ground on which many of our countrymen and many British soldiers fell in the struggle for the possession of the fort which stood on these heights in 1776, and in which they were buried."

The colonel then proceeded to tell his interested listeners how, after the evacuation of New York by Washington's army, General Greene, acting in opposition to Washington's judgment, resolved to defend Fort Washington. On the 16th of November, the British advanced with superior forces from four points. They were bravely met. Our half-naked heroes contested the ground outside the fort, inch

2*

34   SUMMER DAYS ON THE HUDSON.

The fall of Fort Washington.   Jeffrey's Hook.

by inch, from noon till toward evening. At last,
driven inside the fort, where they were too crowded to act, and when batteries on the adjacent hills
were ready to rake them with deadly cross-fires, they
reluctantly hauled down the flag they had so honorably defended. Hundreds had fallen, and over
twenty-eight hundred were made prisoners, and
sent to the prison-ships at New York to suffer tor-
tures worse than death.

During the relation of this and other stories of
the war by the colonel, our party had slowly walked
to various points to enjoy the magnificent views,
"nearly equal to that from the Mountain House,"
Edith said, and had descended to the river again,
at a point known as Jeffrey's Hook. Here, pointing to some mounds covered with waving cedars,
the colonel said,

"Here, too, stood a redoubt built to protect
some obstructions thrown across the river by that
resolute old revolutionary chieftain, General Putnam, to prevent the British fleet passing up the
river. And yonder, [pointing to the Palisades on
the opposite side,] on those lofty rocks, stood Fort
Lee, from near which our Washington witnessed
the defeat of his troops in front of Fort Washington. It was there, that beholding the slaughter of
the patriots by the Hessians, who, with brutal

Washington's tears,

cruelty, refused to give quarter, that the general, who was as tender-hearted as he was brave, was so completely overcome that he 'wept with the tenderness of a child.'"

JEFFREY'S HOOK.

"If ever I become an artist I will surely paint that spectacle!" exclaimed Clarence enthusiastically.

"Then Washington's tears will never appear in paint," retorted Jennie, who always found a mis-

chievous delight in "taking down" her Cousin
Clarence.

A sharp answer rose to the young man's tongue,
but it was prevented by the colonel's "tut, tut,"
and by Mrs. Stuart, who said,

" Isn't it best for us to return to our little steamboat ?"

Once more comfortably seated on board their
gay little launch, our party listened to Arthur, who
said, as they steamed gayly along,

" There was one daring deed done on the day of
that fight which I love to remember.   When Washington saw his patriot troops driven into the fort,
he called for a volunteer to carry a note across the
river to Colonel Magaw, requesting him to hold the
fort, if possible, until night, when he would try to
bring off the garrison.

" A Boston man, Captain Gooch by name, instantly accepted the perilous trust.   He hurried
down the mountain path, leaped into a little boat,
rowed swiftly across the river, landed, ran up to
the fort, delivered his message, obtained an answer,
and then by running, fighting, and dodging the red
coats who held the ground, finally reached his boat
and recrossed the river."

" That man certainly carried a charmed life," remarked Mrs. Stuart.

"Had he been a Roman of the olden time," re-joined Arthur, "the poets would have immortal-ized him with their Horatii, Cocles, and others, whose deeds were not a bit more heroic, as I can perceive, than that of the daring Henry Gooch."

"Fame is a capricious goddess, my son," observed the colonel. "Sometimes she writes the most de-serving names on her scroll; quite as often she in-scribes those which might better be left to rot in dull oblivion; but in every age she omits to em-. blazon names whose merits are equal, if not supe-rior, to those of her more favored sons and daughters. Let this teach you not to work for a place on her roll, but for the approval of your own conscience and of the All-seeing One, and for the good of mankind."

The gravity of these remarks checked conver-sation for a few moments; but when the steamer passed the height which abruptly breaks off at Fort Lee, and was opposite the charming strip of mead-ow, behind which the Palisades are less broken and forbidding, Miss Edith exclaimed,

"O, mamma, what a charming spot! It might well be the Happy Valley of Dr. Johnson in his 'Rasselas.'"

"It is called Pleasant Valley, my dear," observed the colonel; "but the crowds of pleasure seekers

from New York, who throng it in the summer season, prevent its being a very desirable place of
residence.   But for that annoyance it would be a

BULL'S FERRY.

delightful retreat for weary New Yorkers, as would
Bull's Ferry also, which you see just below, where
a long wharf juts into the river.   The British had
a block-house there at one time during the Revo-

lution. General Wayne attacked it one night while
his dragoons were driving off some cattle from the
country below; but he met with a repulse and a
loss of sixty men killed and wounded. The unfortunate Major André wrote a satirical poem, called
'The Cow Chase,' to commemorate the event. In
its last stanza he said:—

> "'And now I've closed my epic strain,
> I tremble as I show it,
> Lest this same warrior-drover, Wayne,
> Should ever catch the poet.'

" By a curious and tragic coincidence the young
man was actually arrested on the very day that the
last portion of his poem appeared in print, and the
guard which surrounded him when he died the
death of a convicted spy was part of a force under
the command of the 'warrior-drover, Wayne,' whom
he had ridiculed so unmercifully."

" I've often read about Major André, and I think
it was a cruel shame to hang such a nice young
man. Washington ought to have saved his life."

This was said with spirit and deep feeling by
Jennie, whose flushed face and flashing eyes showed
the earnestness of her opinion. Edith looked at
her wonderingly and exclaimed,—

"Why, Jennie Stuart!"

" Jennie views the question through her feelings,"

40   SUMMER DAYS ON THE HUDSON.

Romantic scenery.   A fortress of the Evil One.

said the colonel, smiling blandly on his niece.
" Washington would have spared André if he could
have done so safely. But in war it is necessary
to make spies feel that while pursuing their calling a gallows' noose is constantly dangling over
their heads."

The attention of the party was now directed to
the romantic scenery past which their yacht was
gliding. The Palisades appeared less lofty and
rugged than above Fort Lee. Their face was more
sloping and better covered with verdure. The little
cottages, lying in such cosy nooks at their base,
wore a charming air of quiet, which led to renewed
expressions of regret that this lovely little vale
should be spoiled, as a place of residence, by the
graceless hordes of uproarious pleasure seekers from
New York, who make it their resort, especially on
the holy Sabbath. Presently, they passed Gutten-
berg, with its huge lager beer brewery built into the
cliff, like a fortress of the Evil One. Shortly after,
they were opposite Weehawken, or Weehawk, as
the Indians called it, once the delightful retreat of
heat-oppressed New Yorkers in summer time, but
now disfigured by the cattle yards of the Erie Railroad.

" Yonder is the once famous 'Chalk Farm,'" said
the colonel, pointing to a small open spot near the

river's edge, "the ground on which men, led by a false sense of honor, used to meet in deadly combat."

"Is that where the notorious Aaron Burr fought

DUELING GROUND AT WEEHAWKEN,

a duel with the celebrated Alexander Hamilton?" inquired Mrs. Stuart.

"It is, my dear. That is where Hamilton, the distinguished lawyer and statesman, lost his life, through lack of moral courage to refuse the challenge of Burr. It makes one's blood run cold to call up the tragic scene—to see, in imagination, these two men crossing the river with their seconds and physicians, ascend to that blood-stained ground, stand face to face with pistols in their hands, and deliberately fire, Burr's shot giving his adversary a mortal wound, and Hamilton's ball striking the branch of a tree overhead. How such a horrid deed could heal a man's wounded honor I cannot see."

"But I thought Hamilton did not return Burr's fire," said Arthur.

"So his seconds said, my son, but Burr's seconds affirmed that he did. Which were right matters little. Burr was a murderer, and Hamilton, by consenting to the duel, became his accomplice. Hamilton, who believed dueling to be a crime, ought to have been brave enough to decline that wicked method of settling their differences. But let us leave that question. There is a legend about old Hendrick Hudson's first visit to the Indians at Weehawken. Will you hear it?"

"O yes, uncle, certainly. We all like legends, especially of the Indians."

To this remark of Edith they all assented. The colonel then told them that when the Indians first saw Hendrick Hudson's vessel, the Half Moon, they

thought it was a moving house in which the Manitou, or Good Spirit, had come to pay them a visit.
When Hudson landed among them, dressed in a
red military coat, the children of the forest hailed
him as the Manitou, and gathered about him with
reverential awe. Hudson, who seemed to have
been something of a wag, bowed to them in return.
He then commanded one of his men to pour some
liquor from an elegant decanter or bottle into a
goblet. The jolly explorer emptied the glass at a
single draught, and, having had it refilled, handed
it to the chief nearest to him. The Indian smelled
it, and passed it untasted to the next. Thus it
went round the circle; when one of the warriors
made a talk in which he warned them not to return the liquor to the Manitou lest he should be
offended. Somebody must drink it, he said, and
come what would he would swallow the contents of
the goblet. Then, with the air of a man about to
sacrifice himself for the public good, he took the
glass, smelled it, bade his friends farewell, and swallowed the liquor. Very soon he began to reel and
stagger like one bereft of self-control. Then he fell
down like one dead. Upon this the women began to make piteous lamentations, which presently
ceased when they found that he still breathed and
appeared to sleep. By and by he awoke, jumped

up, declared that he had never been so happy in his life, and demanded more of the charmed liquor. Hudson gave him more, gave the others all they would drink, and, in short, made them all most ingloriously drunk.

"This," said the colonel in concluding the legend,* "is the way the poor Indians became acquainted with that fire-water which proved to be the worst enemy they ever met. It has done them more hurt than the bullets of the pale faces."

"And wrought more wretchedness and destroyed more lives among the pale faces than Indian torch or tomahawk ever did," added Mrs. Stuart.

"I think it was very mean of Hendrick Hudson to give them the fire-water at all," said Edith.

"Very mean, no doubt," replied the colonel.— "But here we are almost opposite the Battery and Castle Garden, once the grand promenade of the gayest belles in New York, but now the lounging ground of loafers, and the landing-place of emigrants."

Mrs. Stuart thought it was a pity that the stern needs of commerce should have driven the merchant princes from their mansions around the once beau-

* Tradition locates this legend variously—at Weehawken, Manhattan Island, and Albany. It is not unlikely that it describes a scene frequently repeated in those first meetings of Indians and white men.

tiful Battery to the less attractive uptown streets;
but the colonel said it was all right, because commerce is to elegant homes what the fountain is to

THE BATTERY AND CASTLE GARDEN.

the stream. He then called their attention to the
spacious bay into which they were now steaming,
and which was dotted with white-winged sailing
ships, stately steamers, and little puffing steam-
tugs, which made him, he said, almost fancy they

were offended river gods rushing hither and thither seeking the destruction of the countless vessels which constantly disturbed the quiet of their ancient reign.   At which quaint conceit Miss Jennie smilingly remarked to Arthur, with something of irony in her tone,—

"I did not know Uncle Charles was so poetical."

"This beautiful bay is charming enough to draw poetry from a stone, Miss Jennie," retorted Arthur, who was intent on viewing Jersey City (once known as Paulus' Hook) and Staten Island through his field glass.

This pointed retort put a pretty pout upon the young girl's lips, which was speedily removed, however, when Edith exclaimed, "O, look! see, Jennie, there is a shoal of porpoises!"

Instantly all eyes were directed to the gambols of numerous huge black fishes, now leaping sportively almost out of the water and then plunging under again.   A pretty spectacle often witnessed in the bay.

Very soon the yacht passed Governor's Island, and sped her way into the Narrows, which connects the outer and inner bay.   Here their attention was diverted by the villa-crowned hills of Staten Island on the right, and the less elevated shores of Long Island on the left.   As they shot between Fort

Hamilton, built on the island shore, and Fort Lafayette, formerly Fort Diamond, standing upon a

FORT HAMILTON.

reef of rocks only about two hundred feet distant,
Clarence observed,—

"It would go hard even with an iron clad if she
came between the guns of these two forts.

The colonel said that it was very difficult to decide how much fire a first class iron-clad could endure without destruction, but he thought that, aided
by torpedoes, these two forts, with Forts Tompkins
and Richmond on the Staten Island side, would

destroy any fleet which might have the hardihood
to attempt the passage of the Narrows with warlike
intent. "But," added the colonel gravely, "old
soldier as I am, I hope the experiment will never
be tried. War is inhuman work at best, and the
simple deed of mercy performed by the good
Samaritan had more of real glory in it than the
proudest victory ever won by the greatest of conquerors."

"Don't you think our late war was right, then?"
asked Clarence.

"Our war was ennobled on our side by its object,
my boy, which was to defend our institutions against
the encroachments of a spirit which sought to make
human slavery their foundation stone—"

"O dear, how hungry I am!" exclaimed Jennie,
cutting off her uncle's speech, and provoking a general laugh by the incongruity between her exclamation and his theme.

The colonel joined in the laugh, and pulling out
his watch, replied,

"Well, it is getting on toward noon. We have
steamed slowly thus far, so that we might enjoy the
scenery of the river and harbor. I will ask the
captain to increase our speed now, and when we
reach Sandy Hook we will eat our luncheon.

The remainder of the eighteen miles which

stretches between New York and Sandy Hook was
soon run by the little yacht. She steamed quickly
through Gravesend Bay and past Coney Island,
while our party chatted gayly, chiefly about the
effect produced on the mind of old Hendrick Hudson when he anchored his little craft, the Half
Moon, inside Sandy Hook, more than two hundred
and sixty years ago. They wondered what the
daring old warrior thought of the spacious Raritan
Bay, of the beautiful Narrows, of the inner bay, of
the surrounding shores then indented by creeks and
crowned with virgin forests, and of the cinnamon-
colored natives who came in their canoes to gaze
on his " moving house," wondering whether he was
a man like themselves, or whether he was a god like
the Manitou whom they worshiped.

These pleasant discussions were cut short by their
arrival at Sandy Hook, and the welcome announcement of the steward, " Luncheon is ready!"

Their sail of thirty miles, and their hour's ramble on Washington Heights, had given them "real
sailors' appetites," as Miss Jennie expressed it.
With hunger as sauce they enjoyed their bountiful
lunch, and then went ashore and rambled to the
light-house and to the powerful fort, in process of
construction, at a point which commands the ship
channel. They gazed with awe on the restless

3

waters of the vast Atlantic. They admired the
bright surface of Raritan Bay, with its rippling
waves shimmering in the sunshine, and commented

SANDY HOOK FROM THE LIGHT-HOUSE.

on the gladness with which the anxious sailor hails
the friendly lights which send out their bright
beams from the Highlands of Navesink, which were
visible at the other end of the cape, five miles dis-

tant. Then, after gathering a few sprigs of seaweed as mementos of their visit to this barren, storm-beaten strip of land, they returned to their pretty little yacht.

As they steamed past Coney Island and the Long Island shore their conversation was again turned to old Hendrick Hudson, and his great mistake in supposing, as he did at first, that he had found the route to India and China when he entered Raritan Bay.

"He did not find out his mistake," said the colonel, "until he had sailed one hundred miles up the Hudson, when the narrowing of the stream, the freshness of the water, and the increasing swiftness of the downward current, convinced him that the land of the Orient could never be reached by sailing in that direction. Then, after long deliberation and sending a boat up the river to make further obser-vations, he warped the Half Moon from the bank on which she had grounded, and put her about with great difficulty, she being, as the venerable Knicker-bocker wrote, 'like most of her sex, exceeding hard to govern,' and the adventurous Hudson returned down the river with a prodigious 'flea in his ear!'"

The colonel smiled somewhat roguishly at the young ladies as he quoted these ungallant words from the outspoken Diedrich Knickerbocker's veritable history. Edith quietly laughed at them, as at a streak of pleasant humor; but Jennie bristled up, and with a frowning brow and sharp tone said,

" Uncle, I think that old fellow, whom you call the venerable Knickerbocker, was no gentleman; nothing but a surly, fussy old bachelor."

This spirited blow at the reputation of New York's most famous historian caused a general laugh, which somewhat discomposed Miss Jennie, because she felt uncertain whether it was directed at her or at the historian. Arthur came to her relief by asking the colonel,—

" Why was the river and the island of New York first named Manhattan, sir?"

" That is variously accounted for by old Diedrich, Arthur," replied the colonel. " He tells us that a waggish governor, inspired by some Philadelphia wits, traced it to a custom among the squaws of wearing men's hats. Hence came the appellation of Man-hat-on, first given to the Indians, and afterward to the river and island. This, however, the historian pronounces a stupid joke, but well enough for a governor. He then gives a tradition which traces the name to Manetho, the good spirit of the Indians, who once made the island his abode because of its uncommon delights. Finally, he adopted the opinion that it was originally written

Manna-Hatta—that is to say, the Island of Manna, or, in other words, a land flowing with milk and honey!"

Thus, by pleasant conversation on the early history of the river, interspersed with comments on the many beautiful objects on land and water which met their eyes, our party beguiled the time while their yacht bore them, with bird-like swiftness,

NAVY YARD, BROOKLYN.

through the Narrows, round past Bay Ridge and Brooklyn, up the East River as far as the Navy Yard. Then, steaming round, she glided safely through the numerous craft which were moving about the river, rounded the Battery, and ascended the Hudson, keeping close to its eastern shore.

This gave them many glimpses of the city and its most lofty edifices, and carried them near to Manhattanville,* of which the colonel said, " It is a very pretty suburban village. We must visit it some time, if opportunity offers."

It was nearly sunset when our excursionists reached the dock at Englewood. There they were delighted to find a carriage waiting to convey them up the Palisades to their hotel. As they seated themselves upon its easy cushions, Jennie remarked,

" This is nice. I don't think we could ever have climbed up the foot-path this afternoon."

" Why, Jennie," responded the colonel, " I thought you greatly admired that rustic walk."

Jennie pouted her lips, but said nothing. Her mother replied, " No doubt the path is romantic and charming enough when people are fresh, but weariness takes the romance out of every thing one sees."

To this the colonel assented by a silent nod. Little was said during the ride up the steep hill; but after dinner had refreshed them, they renewed the pleasures of the day by recalling what they had seen, and by planning for further excursions on the river.

* See Frontispiece.

CHAPTER III.

FROM THE MOUNTAIN HOUSE TO TARRYTOWN.

THEIR excursion down the river had given birth to new ideas and feelings in the youthful members of our vacation party. It had given them a slight perception of the secret, the full possession of which makes all travel, whether local or distant, home or foreign, a source of both improvement and pleasure—namely, close observation of natural and artificial objects, and inquiry into the associations, historical and traditional, connected with the localities visited. Speaking to her sister and cousins the next morning, Edith said,—

"Our trip yesterday added to my little stock of information; it has made the creek yonder and Washington Heights look like new places to me. That legend of the bold trumpeter has given yonder drowsy waters an air of romance, while the story of the storming of the fort below has covered the heights with a halo of patriotic glory."

The bright glow of real enthusiasm which lighted up Edith's pretty face as she made these remarks seemed to communicate itself to her companions,

especially to Arthur. Even Jennie, who was thought
to prefer flirting with her cousins and other lively
young gentlemen to acquiring solid information,
caught the inspiration, and declared that "those
legends about the Indians were really delightful;"
then turning to Arthur, she added, "Can't you tell us
another, coz, to pass away the time this morning?"

Just then a big toad happened to hop from beneath the piazza, and, sitting in the shadow of its
lower step, fixed his jeweled eyes as if watching the
coming of some fat, vagrant fly, which he might
devour for his breakfast. Arthur pointed to the
unshapely creature and replied,

"There is a frog—a toad rather. The Indians
called the frog *okogis.* Now, as I don't happen to
think of a legend just at this moment, I will recite
the 'Song of Okogis in the Spring,' if that will suit
you, Miss Jennie."

"O yes. Frog or Indian is all one to me, pro-
vided you say something interesting."

"Not very complimentary to the Indian—but
never mind. The poor fellow has disappeared from
these shores, and we tread upon his dust."

"Sakes alive! as poor old Aunt Mehetabel used
to say, you don't mean to tell us that we are on an
Indian burying-ground, Mr. Arthur?"

"Not literally, perhaps, Miss Jennie. The earth

is too shallow just round here for a burial-ground though, I have no doubt, this hill-side holds the dust of many a brave who once hunted game along these Palisades—but let me tell you what Okogis, the Frog, said to Indian ears in the spring time of the long ago :—

> " See how the white spirit presses us,—
> Presses us, presses us, heavy and long ;
> Presses us down to the frost-bitten earth.
> Alas ! you are heavy, ye spirits so white ;
> Alas ! you are cold—you are cold—you are cold.
> Ah ! cease, shining spirits, that fell from the skies,
> Ah ! cease to crush us, and keep us in tread ;
> Ah ! when will ye vanish and Seogwun [Spring] return."

" Not a bad conception that for an Indian poet," observed the colonel, who had come out on to the piazza just as Arthur commenced his recitation. " But," he added smiling, " you must leave the frog to utter his lamentations and get ready for an excursion to Sunnyside and Tarrytown."

This announcement caused them to spring from their chairs with eager haste and cluster round the colonel, seeking an explanation.

His arrangement was novel, but acceptable. They were to go up to Tarrytown in a large sail-boat. Their baggage would be forwarded by railway to Nyack, and thence by boat across the river to their lodgings. They were to be ready as soon as possible.

3*

As their departure was not wholly unexpected, they were not long in packing their trunks. A carriage bore them from the Mountain House to the river, where a stout sail-boat, manned by two men with hard hands and bronzed faces, awaited them.

A fine southerly breeze wafted them up the noble stream with all desirable speed, giving them a fine view of the Palisades in their grandest and wildest aspect, and bringing them, in due time, opposite the beautiful city of Yonkers, four miles from Spuyten Duyvel Creek.

"Yonkers!" exclaimed Jennie, "what a homely name for such a pretty place."

"Its meaning is prettier than its sound, which is not altogether euphonious, I confess. We got it from the Dutch, who called it Yonkheer, which signifies the son of the master or lord, that is, the family heir. It was originally called Donck's Colony, after Adrian Van der Donck, who purchased its site from the Indians."

"What did the Indians call it, uncle?" asked Edith.

"They, with more poetical feeling than the lusty Dutchmen, called it *Nap-pe-cha-mak*, or the rapid-river town, because of the merry stream which there comes tumbling and dancing down from the green hills toward its resting place, the Hudson. This expressive name was changed to Neperah by the early colonists, and afterward to Saw-mill River.

"O, the utilitarian vandals!" exclaimed Mrs. Stuart with an earnestness which made them all laugh, approvingly of course.

" Was not Isaac Van Wart, one of the captors of André, buried at Yonkers, sir?" asked Clarence.

" Not exactly in Yonkers, my son, but near it, in the burial-ground of the Presbyterian Church of Greenburgh, that rustic patriot sleeps the sleep of the just. A marble monument marks the spot, and records his fidelity to his trust. His memory is worthy of preservation, for had he and his equally noble comrades, Paulding and Williams, been dull of brain or corrupt in heart, our Revolution might have had a termination fatal to American freedom."

VAN WART'S MONUMENT.

" There were many heroes in those days," remarked Arthur.

" That's so," replied Clarence, "but if I do not misread history there were a great many sham patriots also."

The colonel smiled and said, "No doubt, no doubt. Self-seeking men are found every-where and in all ages, wearing the masks most likely to help them gain their ends.

Mrs. Stuart now recalled attention to Yonkers, speaking very highly of the beauty of its situation, of its many charming villas, and its delightful drives.

"There is a little romance connected with Yonkers which may please you young folks," observed the colonel, looking archly at his nieces. "That celebrated royalist beauty, Mary Phillipse, the heiress of the great Phillipse Manor, was born here. In her youth she won the heart of George Washington; but young Colonel Morris, his companion in arms during the French and Indian wars, won her affections, and she became Mrs. Morris. Her husband was a stanch royalist in the Revolution. She clung to the same side, and being condemned for high treason, lost the whole of the great Phillipse estate, which was confiscated by the State."

"Wasn't it lucky Washington didn't marry her!" exclaimed Jennie.

"Why?" asked the colonel.

"Because in that case he would have been a rebel instead of a patriot," retorted Jennie with earnestness.

The colonel laughed heartily at the confidence in

a woman's influence over her husband which his niece's answer implied. The girl blushed under his laugh, but listened respectfully when he gave it as his opinion that if Mary Phillipse had become Mary Washington she would, in all probability, have caught the spirit of patriotism from her husband, and been as true to her country as was Martha Washington.

As they passed Yonkers the colonel told them that a naval skirmish between two English frigates and some American gun-boats was fought thereabouts, and the latter, getting worsted, fled up the Neperah for shelter.

Three miles above Yonkers they passed the village of Hastings, which derives much of its prosperity from the marble quarries in its vicinity. A mile or two beyond they came to Dobb's Ferry, concerning which the colonel said,

"It was from near this place that six thousand British troops crossed the river, shortly after the capture of Fort Washington, for the purpose of capturing General Washington and the troops which were still at Fort Lee. This movement was kept as secret as possible. The troops were to march across the country from Sneedan's Landing, and having secured possession of the only bridge which crossed the Hackensack, to move upon Fort Lee. Had the detachment sent to occupy the bridge secured it promptly, Washington and his men must have been captured, because they were too few to cope with such a force, and they had no means of crossing the

VIEW NEAR HASTINGS.

river below the bridge. Providentially, Washington heard of this movement in season to escape. Leaving tents, guns, and ammunition behind, he marched rapidly for the bridge. The enemy had the advantage of an earlier start and a shorter line; but, for no imaginable reason, they halted at what is now Tenafly long enough to permit Washington to reach, cross, and destroy the bridge. Thus he and his troops were saved from capture, but it was one of the narrowest of escapes—one of the many marks of the care of that superintending Providence which characterized our Revolution."

This interesting incident led to a long conversation about the old Revolutionary war, during which our voyagers passed Irvington, near which is Sunnyside, once the home of that universally admired writer, Washington Irving. Toward the middle of the afternoon they arrived at Tarrytown, where they landed, and were cordially welcomed by an old friend of the colonel, who occupied one of the most sightly villas in " Irving Park."

" How delightful this view is!" exclaimed Mrs. Stuart, when the party, after partaking of refreshments, had gathered, under the guidance of their host and hostess, on the piazza of the mansion.

There was no exaggeration in this exclamation. The view was exceedingly beautiful. It included a highly cultivated park, in which the villa stood, enlivened by glimpses of the fantastic Pocanteco, which rushed, and sparkled, and leaped from down the hill-side. Near by was the village of Tarrytown. At their feet was the noble Hudson, stretching upward for miles, until it seemed to lose itself in the Highlands. Scores of vessels were lazily creeping upon its unrippled surface. Beyond were the lofty

Palisades, sloping down to the villages of Piermont
and Rockland. The younger members of our party
fell into a spirited dispute respecting the compara-

DISTANT VIEW AT TARRYTOWN

tive beauty and grandeur of this view and that seen
from the Mountain House.

"This view," said Edith, "excels in beauty; that
at Englewood is grander and more varied."

Jennie insisted that the Mountain House view

was perfect, saying, with one of her prettiest and most positive airs, " I don't believe there is any thing like it anywhere on the Hudson."

Her mother and uncle smiled at her warmth. They did not know then that some little romantic hopes had been excited and some peculiarly interesting words had been spoken there to her by Arthur. This had no doubt tinged every thing connected with its scenery with an atmosphere of romance. It was, to be sure, little else than childish sentiment, but it had, nevertheless, glorified the place in her girlish imagination.

CHAPTER IV.

SUNNYSIDE.

EARLY the next morning Miss Edith arose while her sister was yet sleeping, and, taking a volume of Irving's works which she found on the table in her chamber, went out into the park to read once more the legend of Sleepy Hollow. Seeking the bank of the Pocanteco, which, as she knew, flowed through the scene of Ichabod Crane's midnight fright, she found a bridge spanning the stream at a point where it rushed with headlong speed over the rocks, and where the seclusion almost made her forget that she was near the busy haunts of men.

Here she was found an hour later by her cousins, who had been sent out to find her. Clarence ran up first and said,

"Ah! here you are, Miss Edith. We have been almost distracted on your account, fearing lest you had been transformed by Undine into a Naiad, and carried down to her royal grotto at the bottom of our beautiful Hudson."

"Or carried off by the headless horseman whose

Pleasant banter.

terrors once drove poor Ichabod Crane almost out
of his wits as he was returning from a visit to his
scornful lady-love," added Arthur with a merry

VIEW ON THE POCANTICO FROM IRVING PARK.

laugh, that was certainly not in harmony with the
ghostly fears which his words expressed.

The demure, simple-hearted Edith looked wonderingly at her cousins as she quietly replied,

" I see no occasion for alarm; I only came here

68   SUMMER DAYS ON THE HUDSON.

Kind words rewarded.   On the way to Sunnyside.

to read about Ichabod Crane, because I thought it
would be nice to read about him near the valley
which was the scene of his fright and flight."

" O, yes; very nice, no doubt, but not so very
nice for us who have been kept waiting half an
hour or more for our breakfast," rejoined Arthur.

" Don't stretch the truth," retorted Clarence.
" We haven't waited ten minutes, and I was only
funning when I said we were distracted about you,
Miss Edith."

The young lady looked her gratitude to Clarence
for his kind words, and, by way of rewarding him
for his knightly interest in her behalf, took his proffered arm, and walked with him to the villa, where
she was cordially greeted and highly complimented
for the bloom with which the fresh morning air had
adorned her cheek.

After breakfast carriages were driven to the door
to convey them to Sunnyside, nearly three miles
below, for the purpose of visiting the home of Irving,
whose graceful pen has made this part of the Hudson classic ground.

On their way they paused awhile to view Paulding Manor, a marble mansion which had attracted
their notice, as it does that of every traveler on the
Hudson during their sail up the river. They all
admired it. The colonel called it " the finest speci-

men of the Pointed Tudor style in America." Mrs. Stuart went into a sort of esthetic rapture over " its picturesque outline, made up of tower and turret, gables and pinnacles." Jennie was chiefly pleased

PAULDING MANOR.

with "the elegant decoration of its ceilings," and with the spacious drawing-room, which she said "was a splendid room for a large party." Arthur was fascinated by its noble library, and Clarence found especial pleasure in examining the mullions and tracery which adorn its windows. All of them agreed that they were fortunate in having a friend such as their host, whose intimate acquaintance with its owner could procure them admission

into a residence which was such an unusually splendid specimen of architectural elegance.

Resuming their seats in their carriages, our party
was driven, through scenery which was a constant
charm, to Sunnyside, the home of the late Washington Irving. Leaving their carriages at the gate, at
the end of a romantic lane, they walked into the
grounds. They had advanced but a few steps when
Mrs. Stuart exclaimed in very enthusiastic tones,—

"And that is Sunnyside! How beautiful! That
porch is elegant, and that ivy, half hiding the end
of the house, is absolutely charming! I don't wonder Irving loved this delightful home."

Jennie somewhat shocked her mamma by remarking, "What a splendid croquet-ground this lawn
would make!"

"Fy, fy, Jennie!" replied Mrs. Stuart. "I am
ashamed of you for being unable to see any thing
higher and better than a croquet-ground in this
lovely spot."

But the vivacious miss did not heed her mother's
rebuke. Before it was fairly uttered she was running toward a green archway, formed by the tops
of two trees, through which the water of the Hudson was visible, like a picture framed with leaves.
Arthur was seen to follow her with zealous speed.

After the rest of the party had sauntered round

the lawn and along the path fronting on the river, which was Irving's favorite walk, Clarence asked the colonel if there was not a spring on the place

SUNNYSIDE.

concerning which there is a curious legend related in one of Irving's fascinating stories. To which the colonel replied :—

"Yes: it is mentioned in 'Wolfert's Roost,' where it is veraciously stated that Femmetie Van Blarcom, wife of Goosen Garret Van Blarcom, being about to leave their farm near Rotterdam to settle with her liege lord on the banks of our noble river, was anxious to carry a certain spring with them to their new home. She was confident they would find no such water here. So with womanly ingenuity she one night stole secretly forth in the darkness, and putting the aforesaid spring in her churn, brought it with her household gods to America."

They all laughed heartily at the ludicrous idea of bringing a spring across the Atlantic in a churn! Nevertheless, they followed their Tarrytown host to the foot of the glen, lying south of the mansion, near the river bank, where they found the spring to which tradition attached this history, and there they drank of its waters to the memory of the ingenious Femmetic Van Blarcom.

From the spring they strolled up the banks of the brook, which poured its crystal waters in miniature cascades through one of the most romantic of sylvan scenes, which Mrs. Stuart declared was "just the sort of a place for a literary magician, like Irving, to conjure up all sorts of legendary creations."

"And to hold converse with all sorts of hobgoblins, satyrs, dryads, and other weird creatures," added Edith.

A charming brook.

THE BROOK AT SUNNYSIDE.

Their guide informed them that this charming
dell was a favorite retreat of its late lamented owner,
as also was a beautiful little lakelet, which he was
4

The hollow that once held a fairy sea.

wont in his playful moods to call his "Mediterranean Sea," to which he now proposed to lead them.

A short walk along the bank of the brook and along a deliciously shaded path brought them to a spot of which Edith was pleased to say that it must once have been a "fairy sea." It was a hollow, shaped liked a palm-leaf, and when filled with the water of the brook, which was formerly dammed up at the outlet, where it escaped in the form of a sparkling cascade, must have been as charming as in our engraving. Then its shores were well wooded, a flock of ducks sported on its still surface, as did also the sunbeams which forced their way through the overarching foliage. But now, alas! its beauty had mostly disappeared. The dam was gone, the hollow was partly filled up, and it required a vivid imagination to see it as it was when drawn by the artist.

"A lovelier spot can scarcely be imagined," observed Mrs. Stuart, after they had strolled awhile around the miniature grounds and taken a second ramble on the path which skirts the margin of the lawn above the sloping bank of the river.

"Just the spot for such a dream-life as Irving loved to describe," replied the colonel as he led the way toward the dwelling in which our great magician of the Hudson spent the latter days of his pleasant life.

THE POND, OR MEDITERRANEAN SEA, AS IT WAS FORMERLY

Their host procured them admission to Irving's Study, which they found to be a pleasant room of moderate size, from one window of which there was

Lowell's pen-portrait of Irving.

a fine view of the river. From the other could be seen the lawn and the carriage road leading to the house. They also entered the little parlor and the comfortable-looking dining-room.

"A delightful retreat, a modest, gracefully-furnished workshop for a literary artist," observed the colonel. "Sunnyside is just such a home as one would expect a genial, poetic soul, such as Irving, would create for himself. He was, indeed, a rare creation himself. I cannot help thinking at this moment of Lowell's humorous description of his character. He says of him:—

> " But allow me to speak what I humbly feel,—
> To a true poet heart add the fun of Dick Steele ;
> Throw in all of Addison *minus* the chill,
> With the whole of that partnership's stock and good will.
> Mix well, and while stirring, hum o'er as a spell,
> The fine old English Gentleman ; simmer it well ;
> Sweeten just to your own private liking, then strain,
> That only the finest and purest remain ;
> Let it stand out of doors till a soul it receives
> From the warm, lazy sun, loit'ring down through the leaves ;
> And you'll find a choice nature, not wholly deserving
> A name either English or Yankee—just IRVING."

"That is a quaint quotation," observed Mrs. Stuart, smiling at the alliteration. " But I wonder that so genial and affectionate a man never found a partner to share with him the many pleasant things in this lovely little domain."

" It is singular," replied the colonel, " but it must
be charged to the extreme delicacy of his feelings.
He did woo and win the love of one every way

IRVING'S STUDY.

worthy of his affections. But she died before the
bridal day, and his sensitive heart remained so wed-
ded to her memory that it never looked for another to fill her place."

Their attention was next turned to the legends

and stories connected with the spot on which the
Sunnyside mansion is built. It was once occupied
by the house of Wolfert Acker, one of Peter
Stuyvesant's privy councilors, and a man of whom
Diedrich Knickerbocker ironically says, "he was
kept in a constant fume and fret by the perverse-
ness of mankind. Had he served on a modern jury,
he would have been sure to have eleven unreason-
able men opposed to him. His house," says the
same chronicler, "was a little, old-fashioned stone
mansion, all made up of gable ends, and as full of
angles and corners as an old cocked hat." "He
called it 'Wolfert's Rest;' but people" who did not
understand Dutch "called it 'Wolfert's Roost.'"

It was afterward owned by Jacob Van Tassel,
who became noted for his patriotism during the
Revolutionary war. He owned a famous goose gun,
armed with which he was wont to hide behind the
rocks along shore and shoot the British, whose
boats sometimes came within the range of his for-
midable gun. He was finally captured and sent to
New York. His house was burned by the enemy,
albeit it was bravely defended by his "stout-hearted
spouse, his redoubtable sister, Notchie Van Wur-
mer, and Dinah, a strapping negro wench, with
mops, broomsticks, shovels, tongs, . . . and, above
all, with that most potent of female weapons, the

tongue." The worthy Jacob rebuilt it after the war, but in size and style more in harmony with his ruined fortune than with its former self.

It was here, too, that Katrina Van Tassel had that notable quilting frolic from which her unlucky suitor, Ichabod Crane, was followed by the Headless Horseman of Sleepy Hollow. In fact, the air of the place seemed to be filled with the spirit of romance, and almost every object, within and without the mansion, was suggestive either of times that are no more, or of the uncanny beings with which the superstitions of our honest Dutch forefathers peopled brook and brake, woodland and river.

So absorbed were our party in talking of these romantic associations that they did not notice the absence of Arthur and Miss Jennie until just as they were preparing to leave. Said the colonel,—

"I will go in pursuit of the truants while you walk toward the carriages."

He did not have far to go, for he found them sitting near the river-side, with arms entwined very lovingly round each other's waist. Their unbecoming position surprised him, and in a somewhat sharp and angry tone he said,—

"Arthur, what do you mean?"

The young couple started to their feet, turned

round, and stood with downcast eyes and blushing cheeks, not knowing what to reply. After looking sternly at them for a moment or two, the colonel remarked,—

"Arthur, I am ashamed of you!"

This remark roused the lad to an attempt at self-defense, and without raising his eyes, he replied in a husky voice,

"We are engaged, sir."

"Engaged to do what?" the colonel angrily demanded.

"To be married, sir."

For a moment the colonel's temper prompted him to make an angry response. But in another instant the ridiculous side of the question presented itself to his mind. The idea of a penniless boy of sixteen engaging to marry a helpless girl of like age rose before him in all its absurdity, and he broke into a fit of uncontrollable laughter. Then thinking that what looked so incomparably silly to him might possibly seem more serious to the blushing boy and girl before him, he restrained his merriment. Turning to Arthur he said kindly, but decidedly,—

"I will talk to you about this matter hereafter, my boy. Run on and join your brother at the entrance gate. Tell them that Miss Jennie and I will be there directly."

Then offering his arm to his niece, he escorted her across the lawn, descanting, as they walked, upon the beauties of Sunnyside. But poor Jennie was too much vexed to be at all companionable. She only frowned, pouted, and replied in mono-syllables to his questions; while in her heart she indulged in such angry thoughts as would have astonished her uncle had they been coined into spoken words.

4*

CHAPTER V.

FROM SLEEPY HOLLOW TO ROCKLAND LAKE.

TOWARD evening our party, refreshed by a bountiful dinner and a few hours of repose in the villa of their host, sauntered out to visit the ancient Dutch Church, the oldest in the State, which stands near the Sleepy Hollow of Irving's well-known legend, and near which they found the modest grave of Washington Irving. The "Hollow" they found to be a portion of the Valley of the Pocanteco. They stood upon the rustic bridge, which spans "a deep, black part of the stream, not far from the church," and recalled Irving's description, which says, "the road that led to it, and the bridge itself, were thickly shaded by overhanging trees, which cast a gloom about it even in the day-time, and occasioned a fearful darkness at night." While in this vicinity they recalled the main points of the legend.

They drew mental pictures of the tall, ungainly pedagogue, Ichabod Crane, who had come from Connecticut to instruct the "tough, wrong-headed, broad-skirted Dutch urchins," and to teach singing

Mental Pictures.

SLEEPY HOLLOW BRIDGE.

to the hard-fisted young men and to the stout, strong-armed, blooming maidens of *Tarwe Town.* They imagined his awkward approaches to the

maiden, Katrina of Wolfert's Roost, with whom it
was his misfortune to fall in love, and the resentful
glances of his more favored rival, the "stalwart, bony
Brom Van Brunt," whose vindictive jealousy moved
him to a ludicrous scheme for driving poor Ichabod
from the neighborhood of the buxom daughter of
Van Tassel.

In an unlucky hour, Ichabod went to a quilting
party at Katrina's home, riding thither upon a horse
characteristically named "Gunpowder." The frolic
being over, Ichabod tarried awhile to say some tender words to the reluctant maiden; but her responses
chilled his hopes, and caused him to leave her side
in a mood which was far from being a merry one.
Then, mounting "Gunpowder," the rebuffed lover
rode gloomily homeward. But when he was within
half a mile of the bridge, "a horse and rider, huge,
black, and mysterious, suddenly appeared at his
side." Ichabod looked round, and to his horror
discovered that the rider carried his head in his
hand, on the pommel of his saddle. The mysterious spectacle terrified him. He put "Gunpowder"
upon his mettle, and rode furiously across the bridge,
trusting the demon would not dare to follow him
across running water. But it did, and instead of
disappearing in a cloud of fire and smoke, rose in
the stirrups and hurled its head upon the luckless

Ichabod! Its aim was unerring. The demon's head fell, with a terrible crash, on the schoolmaster's skull, and, slipping from the saddle, the terror-stricken simpleton fell to the ground. "Gunpowder," freed from his rider, galloped to his stable, and the "goblin-rider passed like a whirlwind." A smashed pumpkin, found on the road next day, might have taught those thick-headed Dutchmen that the headless rider was no other than Ichabod's rival, the bold "Brom Bones," as Van Brunt was nicknamed, and that shame drove the luckless schoolmaster back to Connecticut; but they, being wise in demon-lore, chose to believe that a dead Hessian, whose head had been carried away by a cannon-ball, and who was wont to ride through the Hollow in search of it, was the grim goblin which had spirited the schoolmaster away. Brom Van Brunt, however, kept his own counsel, and, no doubt, chuckled over it with more vanity than grace, when, shortly after, he led the buxom Katrina to the marriage altar.

After commenting with much fun on this old legend, and enjoying the pleasing scenery of the Hollow, our party walked back to a spot near the center of the town, on which the unfortunate Major André was arrested by three honest militia-men. A marble monument marks the scene, and records the fidelity of Paulding, Van Wart, and Williams.

" The act of those three men deserves to be remembered," observed the colonel. " Had they been selfish enough to accept the price André proffered for permission to pass this spot, our Revolution might have had a less fortunate ending."

SPOT ON WHICH ANDRÉ WAS ARRESTED.

"And if the young major had acted more discreetly when he met those three honest farmers, he might have rode past them without suspicion. He mistook them for tories, and foolishly, for his own interests, declared himself a British officer. That declaration saved us West Point, but cost him his life. It was one of the many little things which occurred during our Revolutionary war that reveal the finger of Providence as really as did our most celebrated victories."

These just remarks by the host of our party led to numerous inquiries on the part of Clarence, Edith, and Mrs. Stuart, to which the colonel and his friend

replied so fully that they left the following impres-
sions respecting young André and his capture on
the young people's minds:—

Young André had been sent by the British commander, at Arnold's request, to meet the latter and
arrange for the treacherous surrender of West Point.
The vile bargain had been made. The fatal papers
were in the feet of André's stockings. He was to be
taken down the river in a boat to the English frigate "Vulture." But a cannonade from the shore
had compelled her to descend the stream, and André's guide, J. H. Smith, refused to take him to her
by boat. Hence, guided by Smith, he rode to Pine's
Bridge, from whence he pursued his journey alone.

On that eventful morning three armed rustics
were playing cards under a clump of trees near a
spring which bubbled up close by a little stream in
Tarrytown, still known as André's brook. The men
were volunteer patriots, on the lookout for tory Cow
Boys and suspicious strangers. In the midst of their
game the sound of an approaching horse startled
them. Leaping to their feet they saw a horseman
in civilian's dress, but riding with an evidently military air and manner. One of these men, Paulding,
had on the dress of a German soldier, in which he
had escaped from captivity in New York. For this
reason André supposed that he and his comrades

were in sympathy with the British, and exclaimed, as he rode up:—

"Thank God, I am once more among friends!"

"Stop!" cried Paulding, presenting his musket.

"Gentlemen," replied André as he reined in his steed, "I hope you belong to our party."

"What party?" asked Paulding.

"The Lower party," responded the major.

"I do," said Paulding.

This answer threw André off his guard, and he replied, "I am a British officer, out in the country on particular business; I hope you will not detain me a minute."

Vain hope! Paulding sternly bade him dismount; a command which opened André's eyes to the fact that he was in the hands of patriots. Hoping to satisfy them, he showed them a passport signed by the then unsuspected traitor, Arnold. This, but for his previous avowal, would have been sufficient, no doubt; but now the suspicions of these simple farmers were aroused. They again bade him dismount. He protested, and even threatened, but without avail. They compelled him to dismount, and leading him into a thicket searched him. Even then he would have escaped but for the accidental fact that just as he was about to dress, one of his captors noticed something unusual in the feet of his stockings. A further examination revealed the fact that their prisoner was a spy with memoranda of the fortifications of West Point, obtained from its treacherous commander. Finding that his real character

ANDRÉ ARRESTED.

was discovered, André offered rich bribes to his captors, but their patriotism was stronger than their cupidity, and they forthwith conducted him to the nearest American post and delivered him up to its commander. This sealed his fate. He was tried as a spy, and hanged at Tappan nine days after his capture. But for the unaccountable stupidity of the officer into whose hands André was delivered, in sending information of his capture to Arnold, the latter would have shared his fate instead of escaping, as he did, to the "Vulture," a British ship of war lying in the Hudson.

They were also told by their host that the noble whitewood or tulip tree beneath which Major André was arrested was smitten by lightning on the very day that the news of the traitor Arnold's death, in 1801, reached Tarrytown, concerning which fact the colonel with much gravity remarked :—

"A singular coincidence; a very singular coincidence!"

After giving due expression to their regret that the traitor should have escaped, and the less guilty and personally noble spy should have brought upon himself so ignoble a fate, our party returned to their host's villa in Irving Park.

During the evening the colonel took occasion to talk privately to Arthur respecting his engagement with Miss Jennie. He did not scold the really sensible lad, but reasoned with him on the folly of even thinking about marriage as a near event, at his age and in his circumstances. He closed his remarks by saying : —

" Had you finished your education, my boy, studied your profession, and were you mature enough to judge whether your attachment to my niece be a mere boyish fancy or a true affection growing out of a real esteem for her character, I should be most happy to see you married to her. But since neither of these things are attained, I shall take very decided steps for keeping you apart unless you pledge your honor, after one more private interview with the young lady, to dissolve your engagement, and not to renew it without my consent.

Had Arthur been a silly, hair-brained boy, he would have rebelled against this decision; but being a lad of good sense, in spite of his foolish love passage with Jennie, he pledged his honor that he would meet the colonel's wish. And as Miss Jennie, after a violent fit of weeping, was brought to make a similar promise to her mother, the two cousins, after a few awkward situations, soon fell into their old ways and feelings toward each other. Young as they were, they found by experience that love is not that irresistible madness which is described in unwholesome novels, but a feeling readily kept under control by all who choose to hold the reins.

The next morning the colonel proposed to ascend the Hudson by one of the morning boats to Peekskill, but his host playfully remarked :—

92   SUMMER DAYS ON THE HUDSON.

The name of Tarrytown.   On board a yacht.

"That cannot be, colonel! You must conform
to the traditions of this town as recorded for your
edification by that most veracious historian, Diedrich Knickerbocker. He tells us that our town received its name from the fact that when the old
Dutch farmers came here on business they were
wont to *tarry* a long time, very much to the profit
of those who sold the drinks they loved but too well,
but to the vexation of their vrows at home. Seeing,
therefore, that you are in Tarrytown* you must not
hasten away, for I have arranged with a friend to take
us in his yacht this afternoon across Tappan Bay."

"Well, well, since it is not by the attraction of
strong waters you seek to make us tarry," retorted
the colonel, smiling, "but by that of a sail on
smooth waters, I consent to the kind proposal, pro-
vided it is agreeable to my sister and these young
folks."

Of course no one objected, and, after lunch, the
party embarked in a trim little yacht, and were
borne across the river to Piermont, with its long
dock, built by the Erie Railway Company, running
far out into the river, and its green bluffs rising
abruptly behind its narrow strip of streets. Sailing

* The Indians called it *A-lip-conck*, or Place of Elms, because
that tree abounded there. The Dutch called it *Terwen Dorp*, or
Wheat Town, because that grain was abundant in its neighborhood.
See Lossing's "Hudson," p. 328.

into Tappan Bay they came to Nyack, four or five miles beyond, and greatly admired its situation on the beautiful slope of a lofty hill. Still farther up the river they came to Rockland Lake village, opposite Sing Sing, where their host proposed landing. Said he :—

" If the ladies do not mind climbing up a steep road some two hundred feet, we can land here and visit the famous Rockland Lake."

The ladies all asserted their ability to ascend the steep bank of the river. The yacht was, therefore, put alongside of a wharf belonging to the Knicker-bocker Ice Company, and our party speedily began the steep ascent.

" Pretty tough work, this!" exclaimed the panting colonel several times on the way up; but when they reached the lake, about half a mile from the river, and had gazed a few moments on its crystal waters, which cover about five hundred acres, and on the fertile country lying to the westward, bounded by blue mountains in the distance, he exclaimed,

" What a charming little lake ! The view is worth all the fatigue it cost us to get here."

" What delicious water !" exclaimed Clarence after drinking from his hand.

" Purer water can scarcely be found," replied their Tarrytown host. " It comes from springs fed by yonder hills and mountains, and from little brooks which trickle down their sides."

Their attention was next directed to the numerous ice-houses on the eastern margin of the lake,

ROCKLAND LAKE.

from which so large a portion of the ice used in New York is supplied. They learned, also, that the lake forms the chief source of the Hackensack River, which, after flowing through a charming country behind the Palisades, empties into Newark Bay.

After having seen all that was worth seeing, our party descended to the shore and re-embarked in their pretty little yacht. Crossing Tappan Bay with a pleasant breeze, they sailed beyond Sing Sing to

Croton Bay. There, at their kind host's invitation, they landed and proceeded to the Van Cortlandt Manor-house.

VAN CORTLANDT MANOR-HOUSE.

This unique building, they were told, is a century and a half old. It was built of heavy stone. Loopholes for muskets once pierced its thick walls, for defense against the warlike Indians who in those days made frequent attacks upon the colonists. Its unhammered stone has been hidden by stucco, and Miss Jennie said it had a " cozy, homelike look."

" These Van Cortlandts," remarked the colonel,

"have a history. I think they descended from the Dukes of Courland, in Russia. Deprived of their dukedom by autocratic power, they emigrated first to Holland and then to America. Here the son of the first emigrant of this illustrious house purchased the large estate of which this manor is a part. They have since mingled their blood by intermarriages with the best of the old colonial families."

"These things all sound very nice," remarked Edith. "I think sometimes that I should like to feel that my ancestors were dukes, or princes, or lords of some sort; but then I don't think that would make me any happier than I am now. Do you, uncle?"

"Not in the least, my dear, not in the least. Our happiness does not depend on who our ancestors were, but on what we are ourselves. One may justly prize the fact that his immediate ancestors were honorable and virtuous; but mere pride of ancestry is the silliest of all the forms of pride, since in reality all are children of one ancestor, the banished lord of Eden. The best, the only real patent of nobility is derived from our adoption into the family of the Infinite One, through faith in David's royal Son. Such nobility is, indeed, honorable, and it inherits the privilege of happiness here and in the great hereafter."

CHAPTER VI.

FROM TARRYTOWN TO STONY POINT.

THE next day was dull and wet, and our party, urgently pressed by their hospitable host and hostess, remained at the villa. This, of course, threw the young people much together, and put the honor of Arthur and Jennie to a severe test. They had, as you have already seen, wisely agreed to postpone all further love passages until they should arrive at a more suitable age. But they had set themselves a hard task, as they found when compelled to spend a day together within doors. However, their good sense and strong resolution aided them very effectually, and, but for some occasional blushing and blundering, they deported themselves very nearly as before their hastily begun endearments, which, as the reader must admit, was both wise and dutiful conduct.

Among other pastimes resorted to that dull day was the relation of such legendary lore as they could recollect from their previous reading. Arthur, who was especially interested in the former savage lords of the river and adjacent country, and who

5

had been searching, but with poor success, for legends of the Hudson River tribes, related the following allegory, which had been told in many a Chip-
pewa wigwam in the olden time.

Indian story-tellers, he said, loved to tell of the
wonderful Shingebiss, who could be man or duck at
will. He was a lonely man, dwelling by himself,
seeking friendship of no other Indians, but treating
all who came to his wigwam with cheerful kindness.
It chanced, one autumn, that he did not go South
as usual when the ice-spirit began his reign over the
North, but remained until the ice became thick, and
the weather cold. When he was hungry he went
where the flags grew, changed himself into a duck,
pulled up the flags with his bill, dived through the
hole thus made, caught plenty of fish, went home,
ate his fish, laid down before his fire, smoked, and
made himself very happy.

This content of Shingebiss vexed the restless
Kabibonocca, the god of the north-west wind. It
looked like a defiance of his power, and he said :—

" This must be a wonderful man. He does not
mind the coldest day, but is as happy as if it were
the moon of strawberries (June). I will give him
cold blasts to his heart's content."

Then the north-wind blew cold and stormy ; but
Shingebiss was unmoved. He lived happily before

his wigwam fire, or walked out and caught loads of fish in spite of the ice-spirit's anger.

Kabibonocca's rage increased, and he said, " Shall he withstand me? I will visit him. I will see where his great power lies. If my presence does not freeze him he must be made of rock."

Then Kabibonocca went to the lodge of Shinge-biss, and peeping in saw him eat his supper of fish ; saw him lying on his elbow before his fire ; heard him sing,

> Kabibonocca, neej ininee
>> We-ya, Ah-ya-ya-ia
> Kabibonocco, neej ininee
>> We-ye, Ah——
> I aw reej ininee, aa,—ia,
> Shingebiss ia-ya, ya, ia.

> Windy god, I know your plan ;
>> You are but my fellow-man ;
> Blow you may your coldest breeze,
>> Shingebiss you cannot freeze.
> Sweep the strongest wind you can,
>> Shingebiss is still your man ;
> Heigh for life, and hi for bliss,
>> Who so free as Shingebiss."

Then Kabibonocca went inside the lodge. Shinge-biss, undisturbed, still sat in profound repose. He was calm, easy, indifferent to the cold. He took his poker, stirred his fire, lay down, and sung his song again.

Presently Kabibonocca began to weep. Said he,

"I cannot stand this; the fellow will melt me if I do not go out."

Thus saying he went out in a rage and froze up to thick ice every orifice wherein the flags grew. But Shingebiss only went farther for his fish, and kept on his fire and his singing, until Kabibonocca said :—

"He must be some Minito (spirit.) I can neither freeze him nor starve him. I will let him alone."

"Pretty good!" exclaimed the colonel when Arthur had finished his legend. "I like Shingebiss. He represents the Indian's ideal of endurance. Low as the red man was in most virtues, he certainly ex-celled in his ability to suffer. He was, indeed, the stoic of the forest. He knew how to endure even torture with a silent dignity, which few of us An-glo-Americans can equal."

Our plan does not permit us to record the further conversation and movements of our friends at Tar-rytown, except to say, that the next day, which was Sabbath, they worshiped in the ancient, quaint little church already referred to, built in 1699, the oldest church edifice in the State of New York, standing near Sleepy Hollow. After service they again visited the new cemetery, just beyond, and stood, a second time, beside the humble grave of Irving, the magician, whose delightful pen has given immortality to the superstitious lore of the quaint, old Dutch people, who once owned the shores of the Hudson. Many kind words were spoken of that genial writer, and then, after enjoying the splendid view which delights the eye of every lover of the beautiful who visits it, they returned to their temporary home in Irving Park.

The next morning found them on board a steamer ascending the river. They were soon abreast of the flourishing village of Sing Sing,* which is "beautiful for situation." It is on the east bank of the river, which is here four miles wide. It reminded them, by its extensive prisons near the shore, quite as forcibly of those crimes which spoil human beauty as of that love for natural beauty which had chosen this delightful acclivity for the location of a town.

"O!" exclaimed Edith with a shudder, as the boat glided past the prison buildings, "what a wretched life the poor creatures in those dreary-looking buildings must live!"

"No doubt of that, my dear," replied the colonel; "but we must not forget that their chief misery arises from *what* they are rather than from *where*

---

* So named, say some, by a Dutch trader after the Chinese city of Tsing Tsing; Lossing traces it to Sint-Sinck, the name of a tribe of the Mohegan Indians; others trace it to the Indian name, *Os-sin-ing*, from *ossin*, a stone, and *ing*, a place—stony-place. The latter seems most probable.

they are.   They are treated kindly—too much so,
possibly—fed with an abundance of wholesome food;
not overworked, lodged in comfortable cells, and are

STATE-PRISON AT SING SING.

allowed the use of books and of religious privileges.
In fact, they have every thing given them that is
necessary to comfortable subsistence.   Their chief
punishment consists of deprivation of liberty and
of enforced silence. The latter, no doubt, is very,
very hard to endure.   If solitary confinement were
added to it, as was once the case, it would be fear-

ful. But the humane spirit of the Gospel has made the prison-life of modern criminals so endurable as to be but little dreaded by men who make crime the business of their lives."

" But would you have the State return to the old methods of treating criminals, colonel?" asked Mrs. Stuart.

" Not exactly. In fact, I have no very positive opinions on the difficult question of how to treat criminals. I only think that the State-prison of to-day is not much dreaded by bad men. I incline to think that the expatriation of *confirmed* criminals to Alaska, or some other desolate land, where they would be compelled by circumstances to lead lives of industry or starve, would be a greater terror to evil-doers, and a likelier means of bringing about their restoration—but we are passing Sing Sing and approaching Croton, formerly Teller's, Point.

Every eye was now turned toward the narrow neck of land which stretches nearly two miles out into the river, and divides Tappan Bay, or Tappaanse Zee, as the Dutch called it, from Haverstraw Bay. This point, the colonel told them, was called *Se-nas-qua* by the Indians. An Englishman, not having very clear ideas of the ill effects of rum, bought the Point of the red men for a barrel of rum and twelve blankets. He changed its name

to Sarah's Point, in honor of his wife; but the
public, less gallant than the husband, called it Teller's Point until lately, when the same capricious
authority changed it to Croton Point.

CROTON POINT, FROM SING SING.

Before reaching the Point the colonel pointed
them to the mouth of the Croton River and said,—

"I wish we had time and opportunity to ascend
Croton Bay into the river. The bay, with its little
islet, its miniature inlets, and its jutting points, is
like a portion of fairyland. On a still day and in a
hazy atmosphere one feels as if he were in some
dreamy "land of drowsy head." The scenery of the

Mouth of the Croton.

MOUTH OF THE CROTON.

river itself is very picturesque. I was very much struck with its beauty, especially in the vicinity of the rickety old High Bridge."

5 *

"Uncle, is that the river which supplies New York with water?" asked Jennie.

"The very same, my dear."

"Where did it get its name, sir?" inquired Clarence.

"Tradition derives it from an Indian sachem named Croton. The Indians themselves called it *Kitch-a-wan*, the swift stream. It rises in the green hills of Putnam and Dutchess. Its waters are very pure. They are collected into a vast reservoir, which is, in fact, an artificial lake, six miles long, formed by a dam, and containing five hundred million gallons of water. This flows into that wonderful aqueduct, forty miles in length, by which the people of New York are supplied with water, at the rate of forty thousand gallons per minute. At some future time we must visit this vast reservoir and other great works connected with it. Now, we are just rounding the Point and entering Haverstraw Bay."

The young people were greatly interested in Haverstraw, which lies on the west shore of the river, about thirty-seven miles from New York, because the scene of Arnold's secret meeting with André was in an estuary just below it. The colonel related the facts with such graphic power that the scenes rose in their minds like a series of pictures.

They mentally saw the mysterious movement of a boat with muffled oars, held by a single boatman, paddling out from the creek at midnight and approaching the "Vulture," which lay like a vast shad-

HIGH BRIDGE OVER THE CROTON.

ow on the river. They saw the descent of André from the frigate in dead silence, and the boat moving back to the creek. They watched the boatman as he guided his companion into a thicket, and they heard him whisper his introduction as John Anderson (his assumed name) to Gustavus (Arnold's assumed name). They gazed on the traitor and the spy, standing in the deep shadows of the trees, talk-

ing with earnestness, but in whispers, and with frequent starts and suspicious glances on every side.
They pictured the gradual breaking of night into
morning, the return and warning words of the boat-

CROTON DAM.

man, Joshua H. Smith, the mounting of André and
Arnold upon the latter's horses, the ride within the
American lines, the sentinel's challenge, André's
hesitation, Arnold's attempt to assure him of safety,
their ride to Smith's house on Treason Hill, the
alarm of both as the heavy boom of a gun from the
river below fell on their ears, André's disquietude

when he saw the "Vulture" drop down the river, beyond the range of the shots which were assailing it from Croton Point, the hiding of the fatal papers in the spy's stockings, his passage across the

GRASSY POINT AND TORN MOUNTAIN.

river under Smith's escort, and his ride to Tarrytown, where he fell into the hands of the patriot guards. All these pictures seemed like passing realities as they listened, and so engaged their attention that they started when some one near them said to a companion :—

Hendrick Hudson and the Indians.

" That little village on yonder tongue of land is Grassy Point."

" Grassy Point ! " exclaimed the colonel, pointing toward the west side of the river; " that is a little brick-making community. We shall soon be at Stony Point."

" That's where old Hendrick Hudson had an affray with the up-river Indians," observed Arthur. " They crowded round his vessel in such numbers that he had to use fire-arms to keep them back. He killed one of their number, and that changed them from wonder-stricken friends into blood-thirsty enemies."

" I don't see how he could have done otherwise, though," observed the colonel. " It would not have been either prudent or safe to let them crowd into his little craft. But now we can see Stony Point clearly. You observe there is nothing of it but a rough granite promontory jutting into the river and crowned with a light-house and a fog bell. But, barren and useless as it is, it is rich in heroic associations. The capture of the fort by " Mad Anthony " was one of the most daring deeds of our Revolutionary war."

" Tell us about it if you please, sir," said Clarence.

The colonel, nothing loth, then told them that early in the war our patriot fathers built a fort on

Two famous forts.

Stony Point, and also on Verplanck's Point opposite, on the east side of the river. As these forts commanded the river, the British attacked them with superior numbers and captured them without loss

VERPLANCK'S POINT, FROM STONY POINT LIGHT-HOUSE.

on either side. But seeing how important these lost forts were to the command of the Highlands of the Hudson, Washington resolved to recapture and hold them. With his habitual caution, he first made himself thoroughly acquainted with the works and the approaches thereto. This done, he committed

the perilous task to General Anthony Wayne, called
"Mad Anthony," because of his daring character.
He, fully aware of the danger to be confronted, accepted the command with a remark which was as
profane as it was bold. With only two hundred and
ninety men he marched, on the night of July 15,
1779, to attempt the seemingly hopeless task.

The fort crowned the promontory, as the light-
house does now. The waves of the Hudson washed
the sides of the hill and overflowed a morass at high
water on another side. Abatis surrounded the hill.
The fort bristled with cannon. But Wayne forded
the morass, formed his men into two columns, and,
at or shortly after midnight, moved in silence
to the attack. His devoted men marched up the
hill hoping to surprise the foe. But the sentinels
were wary and watchful. The alarm was given, the
drums rolled, the cry, to arms! to arms! echoed
through the fort. The garrison rushed to the ram-
parts and poured fearful showers of iron hail down
upon the assailants. But, nothing daunted, our patriot soldiers pressed over the abatis, marched over
their own dead, advanced steadfastly up the heights,
as their heroic leader kept shouting " Forward !
Forward !" A shot grazed " Mad Anthony's " head
and brought him down to his knees; but while the
blood from his wound blinded his eyes, he shouted :—

" March on! Carry me into the fort. I will die at the head of my column."

ANTHONY WAYNE.

And march on they did until both columns met in the middle of the fort. The British cried for quarter. The patriots wildly shouted, "Victory! victory!" and at two o'clock "Mad Anthony," not seriously hurt by his wound, wrote these telling words to Washington :—

Splendid fighting.   Two great wars.

"STONY POINT, 2 A.M.

"DEAR GENERAL:—The American flag waves here!"

"Yours truly,   ANTHONY WAYNE."

"That was splendid fighting!" exclaimed Clarence enthusiastically. "I should like to do such a deed if I were a soldier."

Edith cast a sad, reproachful look on the young man. Her mild nature could see nothing but the painful side of battle scenes. Her tender sympathy for the suffering swallowed up her admiration for the hero whose greenest laurels sprang from the blood of his fellow-creatures. The colonel noticed her expression, read its meaning, and said:—

"Edith does not admire military heroes. Her heart is too soft to find pleasure in their loftiest deeds. May be she is right. War is terrible, and is never right except when waged against evils, which, owing to the vast range of their influence, are worse than war in their aggregate results. Our war for political liberty a hundred years ago, and our recent war to preserve the unity of our country, were both of this character. While, therefore, we shiver when we look at the suffering and loss of life they involved, we must not refuse our admiration to the heroic men to whose courage we owe our victories."

CHAPTER VII.

THROUGH THE HIGHLANDS.

THE boat was by this time approaching the most attractive portion of our magnificent river—the Highlands. Said the colonel, as he pointed toward the tall, misty hills from between which the stream issued like some huge *Python* emerging from its den :—

"We are now about to pass some of the finest scenery in the world. For the next twenty miles we shall find this majestic river pent in between cliffs which rise from one thousand to fifteen hundred feet high—forming a gap which suggests that at some time, in ages past, this river, anciently a vast lake, broke through its rocky barriers and cut for itself a passage to the sea."

"I recollect some lines descriptive of that supposed gigantic exploit," remarked Clarence in a tone slightly sarcastic. "The poet says of it :—

"'The pent-up flood, impatient of control,
    In ages past here burst its granite bound,
  Then to the sea in broad meanders stole,
    While pond'rous ruin strewed the broken ground,
  And these gigantic hills forever closed around.'"

"Graphic lines! but I suspect you doubt their truth, Clarence," observed Mrs. Stuart.

"I think that probably we know quite as much about it as the poet did," replied Clarence, laughing.

"Very likely, very likely," replied the colonel; "men may talk with much show of wisdom concerning the ways in which nature did her work in the long, long ago; but they really know very little about it. This much, however, we shall soon find to be true: our course lies between heights in which our majestic Hudson possesses unrivaled beauties. To use a poet's language:—

> "'By wooded bluffs we steal, by leaning lawn,
>   By palace, village, cot; a sweet surprise,
>   At every turn, the vision breaks upon.'"

The boat, after touching at Caldwell's Landing, which lies on the west side of the river, forty-four miles from New York, directly under the Donderberg Mountain, proceeded toward Peekskill, two miles higher up on the eastern side.

"Peekskill!" exclaimed Jennie, "what a queer name."

"It was derived from an old Dutch captain, named Jan Peek," replied the colonel. "He mistook the creek which enters the river here for the head waters of the Hudson, ran his vessel ashore,

THE PEEKSKILL IN WINTER BY MOONLIGHT.

and began the settlement of yon slope on which the village is so cosily built. The Indians called it *Mag-ri-ga-ries*, and its vicinity *Sack-hoes*. It was the birthplace of John Paulding, one of the captors of André, as you doubtless remember, and its grave-yard contains a marble monument to his memory."

PAULDING'S MONUMENT.

" I chiefly remember it," remarked Mrs. Stuart,
" as the residence of the beautiful female spy,
Miss Moncrieff, who, during the war of the Revolution, made her charms the instrument of winning military information, which she sent to our
enemies."

At the request of her daughters Mrs. Stuart then
told the story of Miss Moncrieff's pretended sympathy with the patriots, by which she so won the
confidence of well-informed gentlemen as to worm
from them important information respecting the
intended movements of our revolutionary army.
Whatever she thus learned she wrote down, and
hid the tell-tale papers near a tree previously designated. Her notes were taken by sympathetic
tories, and passed from hand to hand to the British
head-quarters in New York.

Her trips to this treason tree were made on
horseback. She rode a spirited animal, which she
managed with the skill and courage of an Amazon.
But one day, while on her guilty errand, a dog
startled her horse so that she lost her seat and fell.
badly stunned, to the ground. The owners of a
neighboring farm-house picked her up, and, after
conveying her to their house, laid her on a bed. In
their efforts for her restoration they unbuttoned the
vest of her riding habit. On recovering conscious-

The spy discovered.   Her life spared.

ness she noticed that her vest was open, and starting up, exclaimed, with intense agitation,

" Who unbuttoned my waistcoat? Where is the
letter? Ah! I am lost, lost!".

Had she betrayed less emotion she would have recovered the traitorous letter from the unsuspecting
woman who held it. But her agitated manner excited the suspicion of a man present, and he sprang
forward and snatched the missive from the woman's
hand. Miss Moncrieff begged him, with agonizing
earnestness, to restore it to her. But he, seeing it
was addressed to some one in New York, positively
refused. Upon this the lady, finding herself unin-
jured by her fall, left the house, hastened to her
residence, and prepared for instant flight to the
British lines. Her preparations were cut short,
however, by the entrance of a patriot officer, who
placed her under arrest.

The letter was found to contain important information of an intended movement by the American
army. An examination brought out complete evi-
dence of treasonable practices. By the laws of war
her life was forfeited; but her sex, her youth, her
beauty, and the aversion of the Americans to deal
harshly with a woman, saved her life. She was held
as a prisoner for some time, but was never brought
to trial. She was finally restored to her friends.

"An interesting but painful story," remarked the colonel. "Treason, or any other crime, indeed, appears worse in a woman than in a man, because, I suppose, we naturally expect to find a woman, espe-

WINTER FISHING.

cially an accomplished one, on the side of whatever is noble and true."

As they swept past Peekskill Bay the colonel told them that in winter time he had often seen one portion of it alive with fishermen.

"Fishing in winter, uncle!" exclaimed Edith,

with a look of surprise. " How is that possible?
Doesn't it freeze here?"

" O yes, it freezes hard enough to satisfy a Green-
lander; but these ingenious Peekskill men cut long,
narrow fissures in the ice, through which they let
down their nets at right angles with the tidal cur-
rents. Twice a day they pull up their nets, and
rarely without capturing numerous striped bass,
white perch, or young sturgeon. This kind of fishing is carried on from the Donderberg to Piermont,
and is said to be as profitable as summer fishing."

" Your speaking of fishermen on the ice," observed Arthur, " reminds me, sir, of the reports I
have read about the ice-boats used on the Hudson.
Did you ever see them, sir?"

" Yes, my son; this bay, like many other places
on the river, is often gay with swift running ice-
boats and merry skaters. I saw many of the former
and hundreds of the latter last winter, making the
bay almost as gay as the Corso at Rome, during
the Carnival, but far less silly. The ice-boat is of
many forms, but is usually a triangular platform on
runners shod with skate-irons. 'The rear runner is
worked on a pivot or hinge, by a tiller attached to a
post which passes through the platform, and there-
by the boat is steered.' The sails and rigging are
such as we use in sail boats. It is a very exciting

6

method of traveling, and greatly enjoyed by young
and old who have courage to try it."

During this conversation the steamer had approached and passed Donderberg Point, into the

ICE-BOAT AND SKATERS ON PEEKSKILL BAY.

swift current popularly known as the *Horse Race*,
which runs for over a mile through a narrow channel formed by the flank of the Donderberg on one
side and of Anthony's Nose on the other. This
gorge is the southern gate of the Highlands, and
introduces the traveler to a region famous in an-

cient legends as the abode of imps, specters, and
goblins, which were much given to play mischievous
and sometimes malicious pranks with ancient voy-

DONDERBERG POINT.

agers on the river, and with the dwellers in these
mysterious parts.

Of course our party, whose interest in these legends had been rendered keen, and even intense,
by reading Irving's matchless stories, took occasion
to refresh their recollection of these legends while

passing through this gorge by conversing upon their details. Instead of recording their remarks I will quote a few passages from Irving's story of " Dolph Heyliger," and from the veracious record of his immortal Diedrich Knickerbocker.

Speaking of the phantom ship, already described in these pages, which, after sailing up the river, disappeared in the Highlands, Irving says:—

" Since that time we have no authentic accounts of her, though it is said she still haunts the Highlands, and cruises about Point-no-Point. People who live along the river insist that they sometimes see her in summer moonlight; that in a deep, still midnight they have heard the chant of her crew as if heaving the lead; but sights and sounds are so deceptive along the mountainous shores, and about the wide bays and long reaches of this great river, that I confess I have very strong doubts upon the subject.

" It is certain, nevertheless, that strange things have been seen in these Highlands in storms, which are considered as connected with the old story of the ship. The captains of the river craft talk of a little bulbous-bottomed Dutch goblin, in trunk-hose and sugar-loafed hat, with a speaking-trumpet in his hand, which, they say, keeps about the Donderberg. They declare that they have heard him in

stormy weather, in the midst of the turmoil, giving
orders in low Dutch for the piping up of a fresh
gust of wind, or the rattling off of another thunder-
clap. That sometimes he has been seen surrounded by a crew of little imps in broad breeches and
short doublets; tumbling head over heels in the
rack and mist, and playing a thousand gambols in
the air; or buzzing, like a swarm of flies, about
Anthony's Nose; and that at such times the hurry-
scurry of the storm was always greatest. One time
a sloop in passing by the Donderberg was overtaken
by a thunder-gust that came sweeping round the
mountain, and seemed to burst just over the vessel.
Though tight and well ballasted she labored dread-
fully, and the water came over the gunwale. All
the crew were amazed when it was discovered that
there was a little white sugar-loaf hat on the mast-
head, known at once as the hat of the Heer of the
Donderberg. Nobody, however, dared to climb to
the mast-head and get rid of this terrible hat. The
sloop continued laboring and rocking as if she
would have rolled her mast overboard, and seemed
in continual danger either of upsetting or running
on shore. In this way she drove quite through the
Highlands, until she had passed Pollopel's Island,
where, it is said, the jurisdiction of the Donderberg
potentate ceases. No sooner had she passed this

The horse-shoe on the mast.   Doing homage to the goblin.

bourne than the little hat spun up into the air like a top, whirled up all the clouds into a vortex, and hurried them back to the summit of the Donder-berg, while the sloop righted herself and sailed on as quietly as if on a mill-pond. Nothing saved her from utter wreck but the fortunate circumstance of having a horse-shoe nailed against the mast; a wise precaution against evil spirits, since adopted by all Dutch captains that navigate this haunted river.

"There is another story told of this foul weather urchin by Skipper Daniel Ouslesticker, of Fishkill, who was never known to tell a lie. He declared that in a severe squall he saw him seated astride of his bowsprit, riding the sloop ashore, full butt against Anthony's Nose; and that he was exorcised by Dominie Van Geisen, of Esopus, who happened to be on board, and who sang the hymn of St. Nich-olas, whereupon the goblin threw himself up in the air like a ball, and went off in a whirlwind, carrying away with him the nightcap of the dominie's wife, which was discovered the next Sunday morning hanging on the weather-cock of Esopus church steeple, at least forty miles off. Several events of this kind having taken place, the regular skippers, for a long time, did not venture to pass the Donder-berg without lowering their peaks out of homage to the Heer of the mountains, and it was observed that all such as paid this tribute of respect were suffered to pass unmolested."

" Do you suppose, uncle, that any body ever seriously believed in such nonsense?" asked Edith, when Arthur had finished the relation of these legends.

" Ignorance is the mother of many superstitions, my dear, and many of the Dutch were very ignorant. That class, no doubt, believed in some such weird stories, but intelligent people regarded them as we do, though, in those days, many even of this class believed in specters, wizards, and witches. But we must not lose sight of the rare scenery of these remarkable waters while we are talking about their legends."

The colonel then called their attention to a steep valley lying between Anthony's Nose and another almost equally lofty height half a mile below it. He told them that a wild stream, known as the Brocken Kill, or Broken Creek, because seen only in bits between the rocks and shrubs, runs down that rude valley, forming in rainy weather a dashing torrent, and in dry weather a series of charming cascades.

" But why do they call that bluff Anthony's Nose, uncle?" inquired Jennie. " I don't see any thing like a nose in its form."

" Let me tell you what Diedrich Knickerbocker

Anthony's Nose.

THE BROCKEN KILL.

says about it, Miss Jennie," replied Arthur, in obe-
dience to a nod from the colonel.   Then opening a
copy of Diedrich's history, he read as follows:—

"It must be known that the nose of Anthony, the trumpeter,* was of a very lusty size, strutting boldly from his countenance like a mountain of Golconda, being sumptuously bedecked with rubies and other precious stones—the true regalia of a king of good fellows, which jolly Bacchus grants to all who bouse it heartily at the flagon. Now thus it happened that, bright and early in the morning, the good Anthony, having washed his burly visage, was leaning over the quarter railing of the galley, contemplating it in the glassy wave below. Just at this moment the illustrious sun, breaking in all his splendor from behind one of the high bluffs of the Highlands, did dart one of his most potent beams full upon the refulgent nose of the sounder of brass, the reflection of which shot straightway down, hissing hot, into the water, and killed a mighty sturgeon that was sporting beside the vessel. This huge monster being, with infinite labor, hoisted on board, furnished a luxurious repast for all the crew, being accounted of excellent flavor, excepting about the wound, where it smacked a little of brimstone; and this, on my veracity, was the first time that ever sturgeon was eaten in these parts by Christian people. When this astonishing miracle came to be made known to Peter Stuyvesant, and that he tasted of

---

* Anthony Van Corlaer was trumpeter to Governor Stuyvesant.

6*

the unknown fish, he, as may well be supposed, mar-
veled exceedingly, and as a monument thereof, he
gave the name of Anthony's Nose to a stout prom-

ANTHONY'S NOSE AND THE SUGAR LOAF.

ontory in the neighborhood, and it has continued to
be called Anthony's Nose ever since that time."

A hearty laugh greeted the reader as he finished
this veracious story, after which the colonel remarked :—

" Let us pass from a ludicrous legend to a painful

fact. On the opposite side of the river our patriot fathers built two posts early in the war, named Montgomery and Clinton. To capture these forts

LAKE SINNIPINK.

the British marched, three thousand strong, from Stony Point across the mountains to the rear of the forts. There is a lovely little lake behind the site of those forts, named Lake Sinnipink, or Bloody Pond, on the banks of which a skirmish took place that cost the patriots many lives. The forts were

both captured with the loss of two hundred and
fifty of their six hundred brave defenders."

" Poor fellows!" exclaimed Mrs. Stuart.   " How
little we think of the fearful price with which our
liberties were purchased."

" Too true, too true," replied the colonel, shrug-
ging his shoulders.   " Society is a thoughtless monster, always ready to accept the sacrifice of its best
sons, but rarely grateful enough to reward them for
their heroism.   But then, you know, the genuine patriot finds his reward in the consciousness that he has
done his duty.   But a truce to moralizing.   There
is a charming creek lying between and back of the
sites of those old forts.   It has high, steep banks, one
of which is covered with trees.   Its mouth is broad
and deep, while, only half a mile back, it is a wild
mountain torrent, rushing through romantic ravines
into the calm river below.   Were we making an artist's tour we should certainly go ashore to examine
and enjoy it.   It is named Montgomery Creek."

While the steamer was plowing her way past the
Sugar Loaf Mountain, Miss Jennie, who had, with
her usual restlessness, been wandering round the
promenade deck, returned to her party with great
animation in speech and manner, to say,—

" O, mamma, what do you think those German
gentlemen said just now?"

FALLS IN MONTGOMERY CREEK.

Mrs. Stuart and the others looked in the direction indicated by a movement of the young lady's head, and saw a group of three bearded and mustached gentlemen, unmistakably German in aspect and manners. After glancing at them a moment or two, the colonel asked,—

"Well, Miss Jennie, what did they say?"

" One of them said, ' De scenery of de Hudson ish finer dan de scenery of de Rhine;' and the others replied, ' Dat ish so, dat ish so.'"

They all laughed at Jennie's poor attempt to imitate the broken English of their German fellow-travelers, and the colonel remarked :—

"That confession was the highest compliment a German could pay to our noble river. Germans almost worship the Rhine. But we must not overlook the historic points around us. Yonder, at the base of the Sugar Loaf, we see Beverly Dock, from which

BEVERLY DOCK.

the traitor, Arnold, entered his barge when he fled from Beverly House, the scene of his treacherous meditations, after learning that André had been captured. Telling his six oarsmen that his errand was of great importance, he bade them row down stream as swiftly as possible, promising them an ample supply of rum as a reward for their exertion. Little dreaming that they were obeying the bidding

of the meanest of traitors, they put forth their ut-
most strength, and rowed him to the "Vulture"
with the speed of a bird. On her deck he was safe
from the halter he had merited, but, with characteristic meanness, he gave up his boatmen as prisoners! The British commander at New York had
a higher sense of honor, and set them at liberty on
being made acquainted with the facts."

"I think that Benedict Arnold was the basest
man America ever produced," observed Clarence
with a frown so dark that his friends smiled in approval of the earnestness of the detestation it was
meant to express.

Pointing to the west side of the river, the colonel
said, "Yonder is Buttermilk Falls, so named because
the water, in tumbling over several lofty and inclined
ledges, is so broken and foamy as to become daz-
zlingly white. The scenery of the stream, and of the
country around it, though rough, is very beautiful.
There is a village above the Falls, and some pretty
villas, as you see, on the high bank of the river."

The boat was now in sight of West Point, fifty-
two miles from New York, and the attention of our
whole party was engaged in listening to the colonel
as he pointed out the numerous beauties and attractions of the striking scenery around them. The
spurs of the mountains abutting on the river in bold

A picture of unrivaled beauty.

precipices, rising in some places one thousand feet
in height—the luxuriant foliage with which they are
clothed—the countless sloops with their large white
sails, tacking and scudding like flocks of wild sea-

UPPER CASCADES, BUTTERMILK FALLS.

birds on the serpentine channel and before the baf-
fling winds—formed a picture of unrivaled beauty.

"I never enjoyed this scenery before as I do to-
day," observed Mrs. Stuart as the boat slackened

her speed when approaching Cozzens' Dock, a mile below West Point.

"That's because you never had uncle with you to point out its beautiful objects, mamma," replied Edith.

"You think I am a pretty good showman, then; do you, Edith?" said the colonel, smiling and playfully pulling one of his niece's ringlets.

"All ashore!" shouted the captain.

A few minutes sufficed them to cross the gangplank and to see their baggage properly cared for. Declining to ride, because they wished to enjoy the picturesque features of the winding road leading to the hotel, they proceeded leisurely on foot. Their estimate of its attractions was frequently expressed in such exclamations as the following:—

" How romantic!" " What a lovely glimpse of the river we get from this point!" " How delightful this nook is!" " I'm glad we walked up this hill. We should have missed a good deal if we had come up in the 'bus," etc., etc.

After reaching the hotel they spent some time resting and taking needed refreshments. The remainder of the day was occupied by the young folks in desultory rambling round the charming walks which abound in the vicinity of the hotel; the colonel and his sister preferring seats on the

Fantastic aspects of river and mountains.

THE ROAD FROM COZZENS' DOCK.

piazza, from which the river and the mountains
could be viewed in the various fantastic aspects
given them by the changes of light and shade,

caused by the many-tinted clouds and the descending sun. When, toward dusk, the young people came in, the colonel observed that Arthur and Jennie lagged behind Edith and Clarence, and appeared to be engaged in conversation which deeply interested them. When they saw that he was watching them they both blushed deeply. Jennie suddenly dropped her companion's arm and ran to her room. Arthur approached the colonel, who touched his arm and whispered :—

"Remember, my boy, I trust your honor."

Arthur was vexed. He saw that his uncle suspected him of having renewed his courtship of Miss Jennie. He knew the suspicion, though not unjust under the circumstances, was nevertheless unmerited in fact. He and Jennie had been careful to abstain from a repetition of the folly they had committed at Sunnyside, though, perhaps, they had been tempting each other to it by separating themselves too widely from their companions. A little reflection led the lad to resolve that he would deal honorably with his adopted father and treat Jennie as a sister, at least for the present.

CHAPTER VIII.

AT WEST POINT.

UR party spent several days at West Point.
They found ample occupation and experienced rare delight in visiting its varied points of
interest, and talking over its deeply interesting historical associations. Our limited space forbids us
to give more than brief notes of their rambles.

One of these was to the Parade Ground of the

THE PARADE.

Military Academy and its numerous buildings. The colonel's military standing procured them exceptional opportunities to see every thing worth looking at. They explored the grounds, witnessed the drill of the cadets, visited the several barracks, the academy, the library, the laboratory, the officers' quarters, and other edifices. They gleaned not a little information about the cadets, who are selected from the Congressional Districts throughout the whole country, and taught every thing necessary to a thorough understanding of the principles of military science free of cost to themselves, but under an agreement that they will serve at least four years in our army unless earlier discharged by the authorities.

"I don't care!" exclaimed Edith as they sat resting on the piazza of one of the professor's houses. "This may all be very nice: I dare say it is: but I don't like it. It suggests bloodshed, and misery, and death."

The colonel smiled complacently on hearing this somewhat impassioned speech from the lips of the earnest, thoughtful girl, and replied,—

"That remark is very creditable to your *heart*, my dear; but on so great a question as preparing the nation for defending itself against possible war, we must let the *head* decide. For this country to neglect all military and naval provision would be to invite attack from foreign nations—"

"Come and see the big chain! It is in the Artillery Laboratory," cried Arthur, running up to the piazza and interrupting the colonel.

This big chain, which, during the Revolutionary war, was stretched across the river at West Point, had already been the subject of conversation. Arthur's announcement, therefore, led the young ladies to jump up somewhat abruptly, and prepare to follow him to the spot indicated. The colonel and Mrs. Stuart preferring to remain where they were, the young people proceeded to the laboratory by themselves.

They found the chain, or portions of it, stretched round a large brass mortar, captured by the daring Wayne at Stony Point, and two small ones taken from the unfortunate Burgoyne at Saratoga.

"What monster links!" cried Arthur, striking the chain with his cane. "They must be at least two feet long."

"They are made of iron two and a half inches square," added Clarence, applying a little pocket rule to one of the links.

"And each link weighs about one hundred and forty pounds," said their attendant.

"Did it do any good?" asked Edith.

"It was stretched across the river from West Point to Constitution Island early in the war, to prevent the British fleet ascending the river. But

THE GREAT CHAIN.

it was never tested. The English found work for their ships elsewhere."

Just as Clarence concluded this explanation, the colonel made his appearance and proposed a final ramble for the day to the cemetery. The young people readily consented, and, after calling at the professor's for Mrs. Stuart, proceeded to the quiet, shaded retreat where many brave men sleep. As they paused among the graves, the colonel quoted, sadly enough, the following lines :—

In the cemetery.

" Here sleep brave men who in the deadly quarrel
    Fought for their country, and their life-blood poured ;
Above whose dust she carves the deathless laurel,
    Wreathing the victor's sword :
" And here the young cadet, in manly beauty,
    Borne from the tents which skirt those rocky banks,
Call'd from life's daily drill and perilous duty
    To these unbroken ranks."

COLD SPRING, FROM THE CEMETERY.

The Cadets' Monument, with its castle form and emblems of war, stood directly before them. They read the names of the deceased officers and cadets inscribed upon it, and then, ascending the hill near it, obtained a beautiful view of the river and of the picturesque village of Cold Spring on the opposite shore.

The ruins of Fort Putnam.

"How beautifully that village lies nestled at the foot of those rugged hills!" exclaimed Mrs. Stuart. "It has a most charming situation."

"Very. We will cross the river and see it before we leave West Point," replied the colonel. "But to-day let us enjoy this distant view, and also yonder one, toward the south, of Camp Town, West Point, and the noble heights beyond."

On another day our party visited the ruins of Fort Putnam, the view from which they found to be exceedingly grand. While they were seated on this lofty height the colonel pointed out the strength of this post, which was regarded as the Gibraltar of America, and told them that had Arnold succeeded in the traitorous scheme of putting it into the hands of the British our patriot fathers would probably have failed in their struggle for independence. Among other incidents he related one of very deep interest, concerning Washington when he had his head-quarters in the neighborhood of West Point. He took it, he said, from a volume entitled "Romance of the Revolution:"—

"The sun had just passed its meridian, when an American officer was seen slowly wending his way along one of the less frequented roads up the mountain, in the vicinity of West Point, where the American army was then stationed. The officer

7

A solitary rider on the mountain.

was unaccompanied, and as the horse with slow and measured tread moved along the road, with the slackened rein hanging loose upon his neck, his rider seemed buried in a deep reverie. The scene

FORT PUTNAM, FROM THE WEST.

around was one of peculiar beauty; the far mountains heaped up, one above another, against the horizon, and at his feet the Hudson sweeping on with a sweet and placid look. But the thoughts of

the traveler were turned inward, and his eyes heed-
ed not the pageant before them, but seemed rather
to be reading the dark and obscure future, or try-
ing to penetrate the mysteries which surrounded
the present. His thoughts, however, were apparently undisturbed—only solemn and deep. It would
have been impossible for any one to have looked
upon his calm, thoughtful brow, the majestic, but
benevolent expression of his countenance, the firm
contour, though sweet compression of his lips, the
mild, penetrating glance of his eye, and the noble
proportions of his frame, without detecting the
presence of the great WASHINGTON. Presently he
drew up before a mansion on the road, dismounted,
and approached the house. Almost immediately
a door was thrown open, and an aged gentleman
in a civilian's dress rushed forth and greeted the
comer with many, seemingly, earnest protestations
of welcome.

"The family in which Washington, on this occasion, was received, was one he had frequently been
in the habit of visiting. During the stay of the
army at West Point he often dined with its members, and in its head he had at first reposed confidence and friendship. But many suspicions of his
honesty were whispered about, and in some quarters he was openly accused of treachery to the

American cause. To these suspicions Washington would not heed, but having been invited to dine with him on a certain day and at a certain hour, and this invitation being pressed with so much over-earnestness, and accompanied with an insinuation that his appearance with a guard was an indication of his want of confidence in his friend's fidelity, and urged to give a proof of his unchanged belief in his honesty by coming unattended to partake with him of a private dinner, Washington's suspicions at last became fully aroused, and he resolved, by accepting the invitation, to prove at once the truth or falsehood of the suspicions entertained against him. It was to fulfill this engagement that Washington, on the occasion we have described, proceeded to the residence of his suspected friend.

" The time appointed for the dinner was two o'clock, but it was not later than one when Washington dismounted at the door of his host. He had an especial object in this early arrival. The host proposed to occupy the interim before dinner by a walk on the piazza. Here conversation occupied the time, and it soon became apparent to the chief that his host's manner was exceedingly nervous and excitable. Without revealing this knowledge, Washington continued the discourse, and, while he carefully avoided betraying his suspicions,

he skillfully led the conversation to such subjects
as would be most likely to cause his companion
to betray his agitation. So poor an actor was he,
and so often was his conscience probed by the apparently innocent remarks of the commander-in-
chief, that his nervousness of manner became so
marked as to give the greatest pain to Washington
at this proof of the infidelity of one in whom he
had once reposed unlimited confidence.

"The American commander, in commenting upon the different beauties of the landscape that surrounded them, pointed out the spot where lay the
encampment of the enemy, at the same time remarking upon the extraordinary lack of principle
that could induce men of American birth to forego
the interests of their country, and every considera-
tion of holy patriotism, to enroll themselves among
their country's invaders for no other temptation
than a little glittering gold. Before the penetrating look which Washington fixed upon him while
making these remarks the guilty traitor quailed,
but at this juncture he was relieved by the sound
of approaching horses, and as both guest and host
turned to the direction whence the sound proceeded, a company of dragoons in British uniforms appeared upon the brow of the hill, galloping rapidly
along the road toward the house.

" ' Bless me, sir ! ' exclaimed Washington ; ' what cavalry are these approaching the house ? '

" ' A party of British light-horse,' rejoined his trembling host, ' who mean no harm, but are merely sent for my protection ! '

" ' British horse sent here while I am your guest ? ' said Washington with startling sternness, as he turned upon his host with an air of command that awed, and caused to quail, the little soul of the betrayer before the mighty spirit that he had aroused. ' What does this mean, sir ? ' continued Washington, as a terrible look gathered upon his brow.

" By this time the troops had arrived, and they were seen dismounting from their horses. This gave courage to the trembling traitor.

" ' General,' said he, approaching his guest, ' General, you are my prisoner.'

" ' I believe not,' replied Washington, his manner having regained its former calmness, ' but, sir, I know that you are *mine !* Officer, arrest this traitor ! '

" In bewildering consternation the treacherous hypocrite looked from Washington to the men ; the one an American officer, the others seemingly British soldiers. But the puzzle was soon solved. Washington had ordered a company of Americans to disguise themselves as British cavalry, and to arrive at the mansion designated at a *quarter before two*, by which means he would be enabled to discover the innocence or guilt of the suspected person. The issue proved his suspicions were well founded, and the mode he adopted for detecting the plot admirably displayed his great sagacity. The false friend was handed over to the keeping of the soldiers, and conducted to the American camp as a prisoner. He afterward confessed that he had been offered a large sum to betray Washington into the hands of the English, and at the hour of two a party of British horse would have surrounded the house and captured the American chief. At first, Washington meditated making a severe example of the man; but he yielded to the earnest solicitations of his family, and pardoned him."

"That was a very narrow escape for Washington;" observed Mrs. Stuart, "but isn't it singular that so much treason could have found a home in the free air of these grand old mountains, which seem made to be the nurseries of free and honest souls?"

"Baseness is not born in either mountains or valleys," replied the colonel, "but in human hearts devoted to selfishness. Let us now turn our eyes from the deeds of traitors, and view the works of the Creator which rise so grandly every-where around us in this enchanted valley. At our feet is the promontory of West Point, dotted with the Academy buildings. To the left, lying on the east side of the river, is Constitution Island, once called Martelaer's Rock, and now sometimes spoken of as Warner's Island, after those graceful writers, the Misses Warner, to whom it belongs. Beyond the island, to the eastward, Bull Hill, or Mount Taurus, as people of classical taste prefer to call it, and Breakneck Hill, rear their rugged heads. On the west side of the river is the old Crow Nest. In short, there is no grander view on the Hudson than this—but the sun is getting low and we must hasten to our hotel. To-morrow we will cross the river in a boat to Cold Spring."

Our party now descended by a rude, broken path to the highway, and thence to the hotel making many sprightly comments on the events of the day, mingled with remarks on their anticipated trip to Cold Spring.

The next day proving as fine as they could desire they sailed across the river to that village, which they found nestling at the foot of Mount Taurus, and reposing upon its granite bosom. Not far from the village they found a small stream in a lovely sequestered valley, called Indian Brook, with which they were so delighted that after rambling and lounging among its rocks, gathering ferns, mosses, and lichens, they concluded to improvise a picnic, from the contents of their lunch-baskets, under the

INDIAN BROOK.

cool shade of its numerous trees. After lunch Clarence grew sentimental, and exclaimed with rapture in his tones,—

"This is lovely! It is fairy-land! We may say of it as a poet has written of another stream :—

7*

"A fresh, damp sweetness fills the scene,
    From dripping leaf and moistened earth ;
The odor of the winter-green
    Floats on the airs that now have birth ;
Plashes and air-bells all about
Proclaim the gambols of the trout,
And calling bush and answering tree
Echo with woodland melody."

"That's very pretty, Clarence," said Jennie, "only, happily for us, the leaves don't drip, nor do the trout plash, as I can see, except in your poet's imagination."

"The poet don't say that the leaves do drip, only that their past dripping has left a damp sweetness, which, I am sure you must admit, is here. And there! didn't you hear the plash of that trout in yonder pool?—but the colonel is calling us. Let us go !"

"That call was timely for you, Jennie," whispered Edith to her sister; "Clarence had the best of that case."

"O yes, I dare say *you* think so," retorted Jennie with a pretty pout; "you think Clarence is perfect."

Edith bit her lip and blushed at this significant thrust from her sharp-tongued sister, but meekness prevailed over pride, and she made no reply.

The colonel led the party to various points on the slopes of Mount Taurus, from whence they obtained delightful views. They also visited Under-

cliff, the lovely summer home of the poet, George
P. Morris, the West Point Foundery, where the celebrated " Parrot Gun " is cast, and other minor points
of interest.   But at no other spot did they obtain

VIEW FROM ROSSITER'S MANSION.

so fair a view as from the grounds of the painter
Rossiter.

" How picturesque! " exclaimed Mrs. Stuart ; "the
river from this spot appears like a series of placid
lakes."

" And from where I stand," added the colonel,
" there is a glorious vision between Mount Taurus
and the Storm King yonder, through which one

can see as far as Newburgh and its pleasing surroundings."

"But better than all, to my taste," said Arthur, "is the grandeur of these everlasting hills, which shut in the river except at that one point."

Thus each one pointed out what most impressed his or her mind, and so contributed to the general enjoyment, until their growing weariness, and the flight of the unresting hours, led them to seek their boat and to return across the river to their temporary home.

CHAPTER IX.

FROM WEST POINT TO NEWBURGH.

"I HAD no idea that West Point contained so much to interest the tourist," was the remark of Mrs. Stuart when our party, having satisfied their curiosity at this place, found themselves on board the steamer on their way to Newburgh.

All the others agreed with her, and confessed to a feeling of sadness at leaving scenes which had yielded them so much innocent pleasure. But this emotion was, of course, transient as the morning mist which was now disappearing from the river, permitting the sun to gild with beauty the tall heads of the "Crow's Nest" and the "Storm King," and to shed a rich light on the beautiful vale of Tempe, which lies between these two mountains, and which the colonel regretted they had not time to visit. On the east, also, they beheld all the glory of Mount Taurus and Beacon Hill, rising between it and Fishkill.

The Highland entrance to Newburgh Bay charmed them exceedingly. As their steamer reached a good point of observation the colonel said :—

" Here, in the far distance, we get our first view of the blue peaks of the Katzbergs, sixty miles away.

HIGHLAND ENTRANCE TO NEWBURGH BAY.

Nearer, we get a glimpse of Newburgh Bay, with its finely situated city and the fine country surrounding it. Yonder little island is named Pollopel. The round hill is the Little Beacon Hill. Old Break-neck lies south of it. Here on our left is the Storm King, which it would pay us to ascend if we had the opportunity. I know of no view on the Hudson with greater attractions than the one before us."

" It seems to me," replied Jennie, laughing as she spoke, "that every last view we get is the best."

" Breakneck Mountain used to have a profile

almost as remarkable as that of Franconia Notch, in
New Hampshire," said the colonel. " It was called

TURK'S FACE, BREAKNECK MOUNTAIN.

the Turk's Face. It is said that an Irish laborer,
while blasting rocks near by, put a charge under it,

saying, " Perhaps the old fellow would like to have his nose blowed." The powder blew off the nose of the profile, but the face had its revenge. Its destroyer was himself subsequently killed by a blast."

" Served him—"

" Jennie !" exclaimed Mrs. Stuart, interrupting her daughter, " don't put a human life in the scale with a freak of nature. The poor Irishman was a child of ignorance, for which, as well as for his fate, he was more to be pitied than blamed."

" Is not the Storm King the scene of J. Rodman Drake's beautiful poem of the 'Culprit Fay?'" asked Arthur, as if eager to change the conversation.

" Yes," replied the colonel, " and I wish we had it with us. It would be delightful to read it under the shadow of the Storm King."

" I remember its opening lines," said Clarence.

" Recite them, please do, Clarence," said Edith.

To this request the young man, ever ready to gratify his favorite cousin, responded by reciting as follows :—

> " 'Tis the middle of a summer's night,—
> The earth is dark, but the heavens are bright ;
> Naught is seen in the vault on high
> But the moon, and the stars, and the cloudless sky,
> And the flood which rolls its milky hue,—
> A river of light on the welkin blue.
> The moon looks down on the old Cro' Nest ;
> She mellows the shades on his shaggy breast,

And seems his huge gray form to throw
In a silver cone on the wave below.
His sides are broken by spots of shade
By the walnut boughs and the cedars made ;
And through their clustering branches dark
Glimmers and dies the fire-fly's spark,—
Like starry twinkles that momently break
Through the rifts of the gathering tempest rack."

SCENE OFF THE STORM-KING VALLEY.

The recitation of this fine piece of poetic description was interrupted by the arrival of the boat at
Cornwall Landing, where the colonel called their
attention to the sudden contraction of the river.
Pointing up stream, he exclaimed :—

" See how the foot of the Storm King on the west crowds the water against Breakneck Hill on the east! This is called the upper entrance to the Highlands. Our men of science suppose that in the

UPPER ENTRANCE TO THE HIGHLANDS.

long ago yon mountains formed a continuous chain, and that the waters of the river formed a vast lake, which stretched its placid waters as far as Lakes Champlain and George."

" It must have been a fearful spectacle to behold when these rocky hills were burst asunder, and the freed waters rushed in uncontrolled freedom from their long imprisonment," observed Mrs. Stuart.

"I remember," said Arthur, "that the Indians thought the rocky barrier was formerly a prison, in which the great Manetho shut up such ugly spirits as would not submit to his high authority. There, jammed in rifted pines, or bound in chains of adamant, or crushed beneath the mighty rocks, they groaned in agony and pain until the bursting of the waters set them free. But some of them are still here, and may be heard in the grand but fearful echoes which disturb these mountains when thunder rolls and tempests rage. Then they howl, and groan, and bellow, fearing lest the great Manetho is coming to imprison them again."

"Quite as superstitious, but less poetical, were the legends of the ancient Dutch concerning these sublime hills," added the colonel. "They used to sail through this wonderful pass reciting legends of a race of spirits called *Brimstones*, who, having once cherished evil fires in their hearts, and breathed bad passions in their words, were doomed to infest the earth as fire-flies, tormented by being obliged to carry in their tails the fires which they formerly kept in their hearts."

"Poor fire-flies!" exclaimed Jennie ironically. "I never dreamed that the tiny lights they carry could cause them pain. I wonder if the Spanish ladies, who confine them in their ball dresses to flash like diamonds, do not sometimes hear them groan!"

The odd fancy of Miss Jennie provoked a general smile and many little pleasantries as the boat, proceeding through the pass, glided over that stretch of the river, about a mile in width, called Newburgh Bay. Passing the villages of Canterbury and New Windsor, which lie on the western side of the river,

FISHKILL LANDING AND NEWBURGH.

they saw Fishkill Landing on the east, with its village lying in the distance, and its mountains towering beyond. On the west shore sat Newburgh, with all the imposing dignity of a river queen.

"We are now sixty-one miles from New York," said the colonel as the boat was approaching the Newburgh dock. "We must stop a day or two in this pretty and historical place."

Here, then, they went ashore, and took rooms at an hotel. In the afternoon they drove along a delightful road southward through New Windsor to

IDLEWILD FROM THE BROOK.

Idlewild or Shadyside, the home of the poet, the late N. P. Willis. They had noticed the mansion from the deck of the steamer. The chief object of their

A charming glen.

visit this afternoon was the lonely glen which forms
part of this charming estate.   As they stood on the

IN THE GLEN AT IDLEWILD.

bank of the brook, which is one of its principal
charms, they obtained a most picturesque view of
Idlewild cottage, and Edith exclaimed :—

" This is lovely! It is more beautiful than Sunnyside."

" There is more of it," replied Clarence.

" The glen up yonder is glorious!" cried Arthur, who had been exploring higher up the stream on his own account.

Following his guidance, our party ascended the brook to a rustic bridge which spanned the rough bed of the little stream that tumbles in miniature cascades over rough rocks into delicious pools shaded by trees and shrubs, growing in all the wild luxuriance of nature.

" What is this pretty stream called? " asked Edith.

" The Moodna, I suppose," replied the colonel.

" Moodna!" exclaimed Jennie, " what a lovely name!"

• " We owe it to Mr. Willis," replied the colonel. " He found the creek below revoltingly named Murderer's Creek, in commemoration, as tradition said, of a white family killed by the Indians. He persuaded the people that this was a corruption of the soft Indian word Moodna. They gladly accepted his reasoning, and called the stream Moodna's Creek."

" There was both good sense and good taste in that," said Clarence. An opinion in which they all coincided.

The next day they visited Washington's Head-
quarters, with its large hall, which has seven doors
but only one window, and learned from the colonel

WASHINGTON'S HEAD-QUARTERS, NEWBURGH.

many interesting incidents connected with the Revolution, which occurred during that great patriot's
stay in the neighborhood.   It was while he was
here, in 1781, that mutiny broke out in the army.

The Pennsylvania mutineers had disbanded and gone home. The New Jersey brigade was in revolt. The whole army was in danger of melting away. Washington sent six hundred picked men, under General Howe, through cold and snow, to the revolted camp. At midnight Howe silently planted his artillery so as to command the camp. At daylight the mutineers saw themselves in a field completely swept by cannon. They received orders to parade without arms in five minutes. They exclaimed :—

" What, and no conditions ! "

" No conditions ! " was Howe's stern response.

" Then, if we are to die, we may as well die here as anywhere," defiantly retorted the mutineers.

The order to advance was immediately given by Howe, when the mutineers, seeing his determination, submitted, paraded without arms, and gave up their ringleaders. Two of them were condemned, and shot by twelve of their own companions. The blow was sudden, terrible, and effectual. There was no more mutiny in the army, for Washington, having subdued the mutineers, like a wise man, insisted, with success, that Congress should redress the grievances justly complained of by the troops.

Our party also visited the head-quarters of General Knox, a picturesque old house lying three

8

miles west from Newburgh.   They then crossed the
river to Fishkill, where they recalled many of the

HEAD-QUARTERS OF GENERAL KNOX.

incidents in Cooper's "Spy," especially the trial of
Enoch Crosby, who was supposed to be the original
of the Harvey Birch of the novelist.   Here, too, they
were reminded of Lafayette's severe sickness, during
which Washington watched over the young hero
with the tenderness of a woman and the solicitude
of a parent.   Nor did they fail to visit the Verplanck

House, two miles north-east from Fishkill, the head-quarters of General Steuben during part of the Revolutionary war.

Having visited these and other points of historical interest, and sought, like genuine travelers, every good point for enjoying the scenery, both at Fishkill and Newburgh, our party again took steamer and sailed toward the romantic regions of the Katerskill.

CHAPTER X.

FROM NEWBURGH TO THE KATZBERGS.

AS the steamboat approached the head of New-burgh Bay, the colonel pointed toward a rock mostly covered with a fine growth of *arbor vitæ*, and separated from the west shore of the river by a marsh.

"That," said he, "is the Duyvel's Dans Kamer, or Devil's Dance Chamber, of which the veracious Knickerbocker wrote that Governor Stuyvesant's 'crew was most horribly frightened on going on shore above the Highlands by a gang of merry, roystering devils, frisking and curveting on a huge flat rock which projected into the river.' Perhaps this legend grew out of the fact that for a century after the white man's visit to the river the Indians performed their *powwows* upon the rock."

" What were *powwows*, uncle ? " asked Edith.

" They were rites performed by the Indians before starting upon hunting and fishing expeditions, and also before going on the war-path. At such times they built a large fire on the rock, around which they danced, yelled, sung wild songs, and made hideous contortions. Then they tumbled, leaped, ran, and yelled, until the devil appeared. If he came in the form of a wild beast, his apparition indicated ill success; if as a harmless animal, it was an augury of success."

"Poor deluded creatures!" exclaimed Mrs. Stuart. "Their superstitions were born of their fears, and tended but little to the improvement of their characters."

"Superstition never improves any one," replied the colonel. "Founded in falsehood, it debases them, as we may see in the case of the poor, ignorant Romanists, who worship the Virgin Mary with seeming devotion, but retain their characteristic vices of lying, quarreling, and drunkenness; but here we are, off the mouth of Wappingi's Creek, on the east shore of the river. That stream is of great benefit to Dutchess County, through which it flows, and from a high point of land near its mouth one of the most picturesque views of our noble river may be enjoyed.

A half-hour's further sail brought them to Poughkeepsie, on the east shore, seventy-five miles from New York, of which the colonel said :—

"This is the largest town between New York and Albany. The Mohegan Indians called it *Apo-keep-sinck*, a word which signified safe and pleasant harbor. There are said to be forty ways of spelling Poughkeepsie."

MOUTH OF WAPPINGI'S CREEK.

" What a grand word to puzzle a spelling school ! " exclaimed Clarence.

" Yes, very," replied the colonel, smiling at the young man. " There is a fine, if not a *grand* view of the river to be had here from yonder bluff or cliff. There is also a noble institution here, called Vassar College, where hundreds of young ladies receive a first-class education. It is to be regretted, however, that this college stands upon ale barrels : that is, it received its endowment from one who made his fortune by brewing ale, . a liquor which carries a curse with it wherever it goes. Yet Pough-keepsie is a delightful city, notwithstanding its brewery."

"I know a pretty legend about Poughkeepsie," said Arthur.

Of course the party wished to hear it, and while they steamed on toward Hyde Park and Rondout

HIGHLANDS FROM POUGHKEEPSIE.

Creek, the young man related it somewhat as fol-lows:—

"Once on a time a party of Delaware braves came here with some Pequod captives. Among the lat-ter was a young chief, to whom the conquerors

offered life and honors if he would renounce his own
nation and join theirs. This offer he proudly rejected, and was then bound to a tree to be put to
death. A shriek from the adjacent thicket startled
his executioners, who were further surprised to see
a pretty captive Pequod girl leap to their feet and
implore the victim's life. He was her affianced
lover, she said. The Delawares listened and began
to debate, when suddenly the fierce war-whoop of
some Hurons caused them to snatch their weapons
and fight for life. Instantly the Pequod maiden cut
the thongs which bound her lover, but in the deadly
fight which followed was herself seized by the invading Hurons and carried to their camp.

" Very soon, however, her betrothed appeared
among the Hurons, disguised as a wizard and medicine man. The captive maiden being sick, he was
employed to cure her, or at least to prolong her life.
His medicine must have been very powerful, for,
when nightfall arrived, the maiden fled with him
toward the river. The Hurons pursued them with
swift feet. Finding a light canoe on the bank of
the Hudson, the young brave placed his beloved in
it, and, with strong arms, paddled to a nook at the
mouth of the Winnakee, where he hid her from their
pursuers, and where, as fortune ordered it, he found
some friendly warriors willing to help him attack

the pursuing Hurons when they came across the stream, as they speedily did. In the fight which followed, he and his friendly braves were victorious, and such Hurons as were not killed were glad to flee for their lives. Thus did this bold young Pequod and the brave and true maiden of his heart find this spot to be indeed a safe harbor. And, no doubt, when they became husband and wife they were as happy as Indians in general, which, I suppose," said Arthur laughing, " was not such a very high degree of happiness as to make us envious of its possessors."

Edith declared that she greatly admired the conduct of the Pequod maiden, and a very lively discussion on the merits of the young brave followed, during which their boat passed the picturesque village of Hyde Park, six miles above Poughkeepsie, on the east bank of the river, and came abreast of Rondout Creek, on the west side, about four miles farther up.

Rondout, or Redoubt, they were told by the colonel, lies about a mile back from the river. It is the depot for the coal which comes from Pennsylvania by the Delaware and Hudson Canal. Two miles back, on a broad sandy plain, is Kingston, formerly Esopus, which was burned by the British early in the war of the Revolution. While relating this shameful wrong, inflicted by General Vaughan,

8*

who acted more in the spirit of a savage Indian than
a civilized soldier, the colonel said :—

" The ridiculous and the serious often get strangely mixed in the world's affairs. They did so on the

RONDOUT CREEK.

occasion of this raid on Kingston. Some Dutchmen, on seeing the dreaded red-coats land, ran
across the meadows as fast as their short legs could
carry their fat bodies. One of the fugitives acci-
dentally trod on a rake left by the hay-makers on
the meadow. The handle flew up and gave the af-
frighted man a severe blow on the back of his head.
He, supposing the blow came from a 'Britisher,'
threw up his arms in horror and exclaimed :—

"'O, mein Got! mein Got! I kives up. Hoorah for King Shorge!'"

"That fellow's patriotism was scarcely skin-deep," said Clarence laughing. "It would have served him right if he had fallen into the hands of the British and been made to do military duty. He was both a coward and a dough-face."

"You are very hard on the poor Dutchman, Clarence," observed Edith.

The attention of the company was now diverted from this incident by the colonel, who pointed to the east bank of the river, and told them of Rhinebeck and its many lovely homes, especially of Wildercliff, the seat of Miss Garrettson, whose father, Rev. Freeborn Garrettson, is so distinguished in the annals of the Methodist Episcopal Church, and of Ellerslie, the magnificent, park-like estate of the late Hon. William Kelly. Farther up, on the same side of the river, he pointed out Barrytown, back of which is Rokeby, the seat of the millionaire, William B. Astor; and then Montgomery Place, the family seat of the Livingstons.

"The stately mansion at Montgomery Place," said the colonel, "was built by the widow of that most heroic man, General Richard Montgomery. He fought with Wolfe when that daring hero took Quebec from the French, and he died in our unfor-

tunate attempt to carry that city by storm in the
winter of 1775. He has been truly called one of the
noblest and bravest men of his age. His last words
to his young wife, when departing on his fatal errand, were, 'You shall never blush for your Montgomery.' And she never did. But she lived fifty
years a childless widow. Her estate, which at her
death passed into the hands of her brother, Edward

THE KATZBERGS, FROM MONTGOMERY PLACE.

Livingston, is one of the noblest on this noble
stream. It contains every thing desirable to charm
the eye and gladden the heart."

Annandale and Tivoli were soon after passed.

Opposite Tivoli their attention was called to Esopus Creek, on the west bank, at the mouth of which is

MOUTH OF ESOPUS CREEK, SAUGERTIES.

the busy village of Saugerties, and back of which rise the romantic Katzbergs.

The ancient mansion of the Livingstons, built before the Revolution, was also pointed out. "Its owner," said the colonel, "bearing the same name as Chancellor Livingston, narrowly escaped having it sacked by Vaughan's raiders, who, on their route to Kingston, had landed in De Koven's Bay to burn Clermont, the home of the chancellor, which was near by. But the owner of Tivoli not only convinced the officers that he was not the man they sought to injure, but, being good humored and hospitable, he feasted them, and they spared his property, though they destroyed Clermont."

"Clermont," continued the colonel, "suggests the first steamboat, which was named after the estate of Chancellor Livingston, through whose means Robert Fulton was enabled to build the boat which his genius had devised. The chancellor had made the experiment in 1797, by building a steamboat at De Koven's Bay, or Upper Red Hook."

This experiment failed, but the perseverance of the chancellor was not exhausted. He patronized Fulton, and was rewarded, in 1807, by seeing the "Clermont" steam up the Hudson from New York to Albany in thirty-six hours.

"Thirty-six hours!" exclaimed Jennie with an air of astonishment. "She must have been a 'slow coach,' as Arthur would say. Why, our boat does the trip in one third of the time."

"Very true, my dear," replied the colonel, "but the 'Clermont's' passage was wonderfully quick considering that she was the first vessel that was ever propelled by machinery and steam. She was the marvel of her times—the mother of all the steamships which now skim the ocean with the might of sea monsters and the speed of birds."

Hendrick Hudson and the Catskill Indians.

As the boat approached the landing of Catskill, the colonel reminded the young people that they were one hundred and eleven miles from New York, and near the spot in the river where old Hendrick

VIEW AT DE KOVEN'S BAY.

Hudson anchored the "Half-moon," and was detained a whole day by the crowds of natives who flocked to see his big canoe with wings. The scene he alluded to is thus described by Master Juet, who was one of Hendrick's fellow-adventurers :—

"Our master and mate determined to trie some of the chiefe men of the countrey, whether they had any treacherie in them. So they tooke them downe

into the cabbin, and gave them so much wine and
aqua vitæ that they were all merrie, and one of them
had his wife with him, which sate so modestly as
any of our countrey women would doe in a strange
place. In the end one of them, which had been
aboord of our ship all the time that we had beene
there, was drunke; and that was strange to the
others, for they could not tell how to take it. The
canoes and folke went all on shoare, but some of
them came againe and brought stropes of beades;
(wampum, made of clam shells;) some had sixe,
seven, eight, nine, ten, and gave him. So he slept
all night quietly."

The next day at noon the Indians came again,
and finding the drunken savage sober, they were
glad, and gave Hudson some tobacco, more beads,
and some venison; after which the "Half-moon"
sailed on her voyage further up the river.

Our party landed at Catskill, and preferring to ascend the mountain in the morning, found comfortable quarters for the night at a village hotel.

Among the Katzkills. 185

Ascending the mountain.   The Rip Van Winkle legend.

CHAPTER XI.

AMONG THE KATZKILLS.

THAT they might take ample time to enjoy the charming scenery along the banks of the Katz-kill before reaching the mountains, our party secured a private conveyance to take them from the village to the Mountain House. They were thus at liberty to stop at many a beautiful spot, and to note the grand and lofty hills they were approaching from many different points. After crossing the plain, which lies along the foot of the mountains several miles, they suddenly found themselves in a deep ravine, or glen, on a narrow winding road, shut in between rugged rocks made gloomy by a thick growth of pines and hemlocks, and by the clouds which floated over the mountain peaks.

Of course they were all eager to reach the scene of the famous Rip Van Winkle legend. To beguile the time, and relieve the tedium of the ride over the steep, rough road, Arthur related the main points of that fascinating story somewhat as follows:—

" Rip Van Winkle is described as a lazy, slipshod farmer who would fish, hunt, and gossip in the

tavern porch, but who had an almost conscientious
aversion to profitable work.   His neglected home

ENTRANCE TO THE KATZBERGS.

was in the village of Katzkill.   His wife was a
bitter scold, and poor Rip was any thing but a
happy man.   One day he rambled with his dog and

gun to the highest part of the Katzkill Mountains, where he was startled by a voice crying,

"'Rip Van Winkle! Rip Van Winkle!'

"This cry came from a short, square-built old fellow, with thick bushy hair and a grizzled beard. His dress was of the antique Dutch fashion—a cloth jerkin strapped round the waist, several pairs of breeches, the outer one of ample volume decorated with rows of buttons down the sides, and bunches of ribbon at the knees. He bore what appeared to be a liquor keg on his shoulder, the sight of which inclined Rip to obey his sign to follow and assist in carrying the load.

"After slowly toiling up a narrow ravine, the mysterious stranger led the wondering Dutchman into a gloomy glen. There he saw a number of odd-bearded men with broad faces, small, piggish eyes, and peculiar noses, playing nine-pins. They all wore enormous breeches, and looked like a set of Dutchmen of the olden time. They stared at Rip in grave silence until his knees trembled through fear. Then his companion bade him pass the contents of the keg round among the company. In doing this Rip slyly tasted the liquor, liked it, drank again and again, until it overpowered his senses and he fell asleep.

"On awakening, he found himself on the spot where he had first seen the old man of the glen.

He rubbed his eyes—it was a bright Sunday morning. He recalled the events which preceded his
slumber, concluded he had slept all night, and tried
to invent some excuse to satisfy the cross Mrs. Van
Winkle. Looking for his gun, he found its stock
worm-eaten, its lock falling off, its barrel rusty. His
dog was gone. He whistled for him, but he did not
obey the call. Rising from his grassy seat, he found
his joints stiff, and his limbs slow of movement.
He searched for the glen in which he had waited on
the mysterious nine-pin players, but could not find
it. Perplexed and hungry, he descended the mountain to the village. People stared at him as he approached, but no one knew him. They were all
strangers. The village children hooted after him,
and pointed to his gray beard, which, to his surprise,
had grown a foot long. The houses, too, were
changed. Strange names were on the signs over
the stores. Every thing was strange, and poor Rip
said to himself: 'That flagon last night has addled
my poor head sadly.'

" Proceeding to his own house, he found it in ruins ;
an old hungry dog growled at him, and Rip sighed,
' My very dog has forgotten me.'

" He went to the village tavern, but that, too,
was old and rickety. A strange flag, the stars and
stripes, waved on a naked pole before it, and

beneath the ruby face of old King George, painted on its sign, was written, 'General Washington.'
The crowd on the stoop was made up of very different persons from those who formerly sat there, and
their talk about Congress, Federals, and Democrats,
was like gibberish in his ears. His replies to their
questions led them to view him with suspicion, and
to think of putting him under arrest. Happily,
however, a comely young woman, who called her
little son by the name of Rip, led the puzzled old
man to question her. She told him that she was
the daughter of a man named Rip Van Winkle,
who had strangely disappeared twenty years ago,
and whose fate no one knew. His dog had come
home, his wife had died, and the speaker, his daughter, had married a man named Gardenier.

"Upon this old Rip made himself known. An
aged woman then came forward and recognized him.
Next, old Peter Vanderdonk identified him. Finally, the good people generally admitted that he
was old Rip, listened to his strange story, and accepted old Peter's explanation, to wit: that the
Katzkill Mountains were haunted, and that once in
twenty years old Hendrick Hudson, with his crew
of the 'Half-moon,' kept a kind of vigil among
them. Tradition said that he did this as the guard-
ian of the great river which was called by his name.

And to this day, the old Dutch people never hear thunder in the summer without remarking: ' There's old Hendrick Hudson and his crew at their game of nine-pins again."

" Very well told, my boy," observed the colonel when Arthur concluded, " but the story loses half its charm in any other than the words of the incomparable Irving."

" Your compliment, brother, is like honey with a bee's sting in it," remarked Mrs. Stuart laughing. Then turning to Arthur, she added, " Never mind, Arthur. You gave us the main points of the legend. Now tell us, if you can recollect them, the traditions of the Indians respecting these mysterious mountains."

Arthur, after playfully thanking the lady for extracting the sting from the colonel's compliment, related the substance of the Indian legends, recorded by that most veracious of historians, Diedrich Knickerbocker, somewhat as follows :—

" The Indians believed these mountains to be the abode of spirits which regulated the weather. They were ruled by their mother, an aged squaw, whose home was in their highest peak. She had charge of the doors of day and night, which she opened and shut at the proper hours. She hung up the new moons in the skies, and cut up the old ones

into stars. She spun the summer clouds out of
cobwebs and dew, and sent them off like flakes of
cotton into the air to be melted by the sun into
rain. If displeased, however, she would brew up
clouds black as ink, sitting in the midst of them
like a bottle-bellied spider in its web. With these
clouds she deluged the valleys and spread desola-
tion through the corn-fields.

"In the olden times the Indians said a mischievous spirit lived in the wildest part of these
mountains, near a great rock known as the Garden
Rock. Sometimes he would put on the form of a
bear, a deer, or a panther, and lead the red hunter
on a long and weary chase through tangled forests
and among rugged rocks. Finally, he would suddenly disappear, shouting 'Ho! ho!' when the poor
tired hunter would be terrified at finding himself
standing on the brink of a beetling precipice or
raging torrent.

"There is a lake near Garden Rock where the
water-snakes bask in the sun on the leaves of the
pond-lilies which float on its surface. No Indian
dare venture near this awful spot. But one day a
hunter, having lost his way, came to the Manitou's
Rock, and seeing a number of gourds lying in the
crotches of the trees, seized one and made off with
it. In his haste he let it fall among the rocks.

Instantly a mighty stream gushed forth, washed him away among the precipices, and dashed him to pieces. The stream kept on until it reached the Hudson. It floweth still, and is the identical stream known by the name of Katers-kill."

"Rip Van Winkle's Cabin!" shouted the driver as he drew up before a little cottage standing in a pleasant nook half-way between the plain and the Mountain House.

The youthful members of the party sprang from the carriage, and looked round in the vain endeavor to locate the spot on which the goblins played their game of nine-pins. Rip's sleeping place was identified by the hollow stone which was his pillow during that long sleep of twenty years—at least, so said the driver, who was very much disgusted when the young folks laughed most irreverently at his solemn assurance that the stone was really worn hollow by the continuous pressure of old Rip's head.

After exploring this legendary nook they resumed their slow journey up the steep mountain road, frequently stopping to enjoy the rich panoramic views of the distant country afforded by gaps in the mountains. At one point they experienced a thrill of rare delight, followed by a sudden disappointment. This was at a turn in the road which revealed the stately looking Mountain House apparently just before them.

"See, there is the Mountain House!" exclaimed Jennie. "How grand it appears! It is like an Italian palace perched on a rock."

"I'm glad we're there," sighed Edith; "I'm so weary."

"Push on, driver!" cried Clarence; "I'm hungry enough to eat one of the wild cats which gave these mountains their name."

"Get up!" responded the driver with a leer which the colonel only understood, for he was the only one of the party who had ever traveled that road before.

On toiled the wagon into a road more crooked and hilly than ever, the grand hotel disappeared, and Jennie spoke the feelings of her companions when she said :—

"Well, this is too bad. I thought we were at the Mountain House just now, and here we are seemingly as far from it as ever. I almost believe that this is enchanted ground, and that the view we had of the hotel was the conjuration of some mischievous goblin of the woods."

"Well, that is real anyhow," cried Clarence when, after riding some time in silence, they found themselves on the grand rock platform, twenty-seven

9

A vast and beautiful view.

KATERS-KILL FALLS.

hundred feet above the level of the river, upon
which the hotel is built.

The landscape, as viewed from the piazza of the
Mountain House, was vast, grand, and beautiful.
A sea of woods rolled at their feet; the Hud-
son wound, like a long silver thread, through its

lovely valley; mountains, vales, forests, and cities filled what seemed to be measureless space, bounded on one side by the glitter of the Atlantic's waves, and on the other by the green hills of Vermont. This peerless view, the pure atmosphere, the refreshing mountain air, more than repaid them for the toil of the ascent.

The next day our party visited the Katers-kill Falls, which they found about two miles from their hotel, but which, owing to the dry weather, were not in a condition to fill the ideal previously cherished by those of the party who had read the description of them given by Cooper's Leatherstocking, in his "Pioneers." In fact they were dry, except when the water was turned on by their proprietor, who, for the accommodation of summer visitors, has dammed up the overflow of the little lakes which are their source. To be seen as in the illustration, they must be visited in early spring or after the autumnal rains.

But if the falls disappointed our visitors, other features of those glorious mountains did not. A drive down the mountain to Palensville gave them great satisfaction. At a point called the "Clove" they saw the Katers-kill rushing into a seething gulf between rocks, which appear to have been cleft asunder in some violent paroxysm of nature. It is named the "Fawn's Leap" because, as tradition

THE FAWN'S LEAP.

says, a fawn, closely pursued by a hunter and his dog, once leaped across the chasm. The dog tried the same leap, but, falling into the gulf below, was drowned.

A little below the Fawn's Leap they found a wild,

A romantic road.

SCENE NEAR PALENSVILLE.

romantic road at the foot of a precipice. Crossing
the stream by the rustic bridge which spans it, they
followed this road for half a mile, along a shelf cut
in the mountain side two hundred feet above the
dashing little river. On the opposite side a mountain wall towered still higher, until it rose a thou-

sand feet above their heads, while the stream itself seemed to have plunged into the unknown recesses of the gorge below. At the mouth of this fearful gorge they found the picturesque village of Palens-ville, and near by the lovely plain which lies between the river and the mountains.

So delighted was the entire party with the weird and romantic scenery of the "Clove" that they returned to the Mountain House, from whence they made trips to Stony Clove, to Planterkill Clove, and even dared the toilsome ascent of the High Peak. As they had abundant time, vigorous health, exuberant spirits, and a constantly growing taste for the sublime and beautiful scenery of these fascinating mountains, their pleasure was increased by each succeeding day's explorations. When the morning fixed for their departure arrived, some of them became quite sentimental in the tone of their regrets at leaving a spot which had yielded them so much innocent delight. Edith actually sighed as, standing upon the piazza of the hotel, she said :—

"Farewell, scene of loveliness! I don't wonder Miss Martineau said of you, 'I had rather have missed the Hawk's Nest, the Prairies, the Mississippi, and even Niagara, than this!'"

"Ha, ha, ha! I declare there is a tear in our Edith's eye!" exclaimed the laughing Jennie.

" I wonder if tears never fill Miss Jennie's eyes,"
replied Clarence, who was always quick to defend
his favorite cousin.

" I think I could make her cry the least bit in the
world over the poor Indian's fate," said Arthur.
Then, turning to the now scornful girl, he added,
" I will try it.   Just think, Miss Jennie, that when
old Hendrick Hudson first saw these grand mountains thousands of red men lived, fished, and hunted
in happy freedom among them.   Now, alas !—

> " ' Cold is the hearth within their bowers !
>   And should we thither roam,
>   Its echoes and its empty tread
>   Would sound like echoes from the dead !
>   And 'mid yon mountains blue,
>   Whose streams a kindred nation quaff'd,
>   When side by side in battle true
>   A thousand warriors drew the shaft,—
>   Ah ! there in desolation cold,
>   The desert serpent dwells alone,
>   The grass o'ergrows each moldering bone,
>   And 'mid their vacant camp—ah ! there
>   The silence dwells of dark despair.' "

" Stage ready ! " shouted a clear, ringing voice,
and Jennie, struck by the ludicrous contrast between the stately sentiment of Arthur's quotation
and this unpoetical announcement, fulfilled his
promise to make her shed tears by fairly laughing
until she cried.

CHAPTER XII.

FROM THE KATZKILLS TO ALBANY.

" THAT was a break-neck drive down the mountain," said Clarence, somewhat indignantly,
after our party found itself on board the steamer
which was to convey them to Albany.

" Mountain drivers never spare coaches or horses

VIEW FROM THE PROMENADE, HUDSON.

in going down hill," replied the colonel, " yet it is
very rarely that they meet with accidents. But let

us look out for the city of Hudson, which is only four miles above Katzkill, on the east bank of the river."

All eyes were then turned toward Hudson, which soon appeared seated on a bluff called the promenade, about fifty feet above the river, and running back for a mile or more up a beautiful slope to Prospect Hill. The colonel told them that Hudson is at the head of *ship* navigation, and is a very thrifty city, which was settled by Quakers, chiefly from the barren island of Nantucket, nearly a hundred years ago. He regretted that the plan of their tour did not permit them to land and visit the fine surrounding country, especially Columbia and Lebanon Springs."

"Lebanon! Isn't that a Shaker settlement, sir?" asked Clarence.

"Yes; two miles from the springs some five hundred Shakers own ten thousand acres of highly cultivated land. They call their settlement New Lebanon."

"What are *Shakers*, sir?" inquired Arthur.

"Followers of one Ann Lee, an English woman, the wife of a blacksmith, and the mother of several children. But she by some means or other became a fanatic, imagined herself a sort of female Christ, and taught that marriage was a sinful state. As

9*

The Shakers of Lebanon.

almost all fanatics do, she soon found followers ; but
being persecuted in England, she came to America
with a few disciples, and founded a Church a few
miles from Albany.   There she died, but, strange
as it may seem, her cause lived and grew.   There
are some eighteen communities of her followers, of
which New Lebanon is the chief.   With all their
fanatical notions, they are a simple, honest, industrious people.   Their worship consists chiefly of singing and dancing, both of which are odd enough to
excite smiles in the beholders, who are, however,

VIEW NEAR THE OVERSLAUGH.

generally restrained from indecorum by the gravity
and apparent earnestness of the dancers."

Less romantic aspects of the river.

Comment on this story of the Shakers filled up their time as they steamed on past Stuyvesant Falls and Stockport on the east, and Coxsackie on the west, bank. As they neared Albany their boat grounded for a short time on the Overslaugh, a shifting sand-bar, caused by streams which deposit their sands in the bed of the river.

Eight miles below Albany, on the east bank, they saw the pretty village of Castleton, so named from the fact that the Dutch built their first fort, in 1614, upon an island at the mouth of the romantic Nor-manskill, which has its rise in the valleys of the noble Helderbergs.

From this point they found the river losing its "strikingly bold character." Instead of beetling cliffs frowning darkly on the rolling stream, wooded uplands sloping into lofty peaks, and naked pali-sades shutting out the view, they found the river dotted with numerous islands, the channel rapidly narrowing, and the emerald shores sloping gently back into the interior. It seemed tame after their recent wanderings among the towering heights of the Katzbergs.

But their attention was soon diverted from the river to the imposing old city of Albany, reposing in quiet stateliness on the west bank of the river, one hundred and forty-five miles from New York.

" The oldest city in the union except Jamestown, in Virginia," said the colonel, as the place came fully under the eyes of the party. " It was first called Beaverwyck, then Williamstadt, and, finally, Albany, in honor of the Duke of York and Albany, afterward James II. It is a very thriving city, connected with the ocean by the noble Hudson, and with our vast inland lakes and boundless western country by canals and railroads. It is rich in money, in churches, in literary institutions. It has a university of high character, a successful State normal

DUDLEY OBSERVATORY.

school, a medical college of superior grade, a valuable State library, splendid collections in natural history, geology, history, and agriculture. It has also a very superior observatory, called the Dudley Observatory, which, among other places of interest, we must not fail to visit during our brief stay."

The bustle that precedes landing from a great steamer precluded further conversation, which was not resumed until after they had refreshed themselves at the sumptuous tables of the Delavan House, and had come together in the private parlor which the colonel had engaged for his party.

"I remember," said Mrs. Stuart, after their plans for the morrow had been discussed, "reading a charming little work by a Mrs. Grant, entitled 'Memoirs of an American Lady,' which gives a very delightful account of the manners of the Albanians in the times preceding the Revolution. According to her showing it was a perfect Arcadia.

"Please tell us about it, mamma?" said Edith.

"Yes, do, mamma, please," added Jennie.

Thus urged, Mrs. Stuart gave her recollections of Mrs. Grant's book, which were in substance as follows :—

"The site of the city of Albany was originally granted to a gentleman named Van Rensselaer by the States of Holland. His title made him owner of a vast tract running from the church, in the center of the town, twelve miles in every direction—a princi-

pality in fact. Portions of these lands he leased to
settlers 'as long as water runs and grass grows,' on
condition of receiving the 'tenth sheaf of every
kind of grain the ground produced.'

"Under these leases the settlers rapidly increased.
Many of them were from families of mark in Holland. The town spread out at first along the river
bank, and then up the hills behind it. Its inhabitants prospered abundantly. They were industrious
from necessity. Their manners were simple without being rude, plain without vulgarity. Their religious life was stiff and formal, yet it was productive of social order and morality. In the absence
of schools, mothers were the teachers of their children. In addition to this, and their household duties,
they, with their daughters, cultivated the garden,
with which every house was surrounded, and 'into
which no foot of man entered after they were dug
in spring.' With her great calash on her head, her
little painted basket of seeds on her arm, and her
rake over her shoulder, the mistress of a household
would enter her garden and sow, plant, and rake
incessantly. These fair gardeners were great and
very successful florists.

"The summer evenings were devoted to sociability
by these unsophisticated people. Then nearly every
porch was filled. At one door young matrons, at

another the elders of the people, at a third the youths and maidens gayly chatting or singing, while the children played round the trees, or waited by the cows for the milk which was the chief ingredient of their frugal supper, a meal which they generally ate sitting on the steps in the open air.

"For amusements the young men hunted and

SLEIGH RIDING ON THE HUDSON.

fished, the girls visited each other. In spring and summer both sexes made frequent rural excursions, enjoying picnics in the grand old woods, to which the young men contributed fish and birds, and the young ladies doughnuts, pies, and other products of their culinary skill. In winter skating, sleighing, especially on the river, and coasting, afforded them abundance of healthy and delightful entertainment, as they do to the young folks of the present generation.

"In that primitive society the people married young, as they could safely and wisely do, because their wants were few, small outfits sufficed, and they were sure of comfortable support from the fruits of that industry to which they had all been trained.

"A peculiar frolic, popular with young Albanians, but which can scarcely be considered moral, however, was very common in those old days. They would sometimes spend a convivial evening at a tavern, on which occasions they made it a point 'to steal either a roasting pig or a fat turkey' for their supper. No one in Albany ever feared the loss of any other species of property except these animals, which, in consequence of this mischievous practice, were guarded by their owner with great care.

"Mrs. Grant records one ludicrous incident connected with this highly censurable practice. It seems that two parties, unknown to each other, had resolved one evening to steal the same roasting pig. One of them happening to be first in the field secured the pig and carried it with all possible speed to the 'King's Arms' to be cooked for their supper. When the second party found the pig gone they shrewdly guessed its fate, and their leader, bidding them wait for him at a rival tavern, hurried to the 'King's Arms.' There this gay, unscrupulous youth penetrated the kitchen, saw the pig roasting before the fire, and found out, by questioning the sable cook, for whom she was preparing supper. He then sent the unsuspecting Dinah with a message to one of the pig-stealers. No sooner was she out of the room than this young roysterer cut the string by which the animal was suspended before the blazing fire, and laying the savory creature in the dripping pan, ran with it to his expectant friends at the other tavern, and ordered its roasting to be completed for the supper.

"Meantime the party at the 'King's Arms,' learning their disaster, readily guessed both the trick and its authors. They also speedily devised a counter-trick by which to recover possession of the lost pig. Quietly collecting some dry brush, they placed it in front of the rival tavern. Setting it on fire, they shouted 'Fire! fire!' most lustily. This cry, so alarming in a village built chiefly of wood, and unprovided with engines for extinguishing fires, quickly drew every person in the tavern to the door. Seizing this opportunity, the purveyor of the 'King's Arms' party stole into the kitchen, and carrying the pig out by the back door, returned to his friends rejoicing over the recovery of their spoils."

"A very amusing, if not a commendable, fact," observed the colonel as Mrs. Stuart concluded amid the laughter of the young folk. " It only proves, however, that some, at least, of the Albany boys owed their morality quite as much to their circumstances as to their principles. Opportunity would have made those pig-stealers as *fast* as only too many of our young city people are in these degenerate times."

"You are very severe on the young gentlemen, uncle," remarked Edith.

" No more so than facts warrant, my dear," replied Mrs. Stuart. " I recollect Mrs. Grant states that when portions of the British army made its appearance in Albany during the French wars, the young Albanians of both sexes speedily trampled on the counsels of their elders, and, to the great distress of their good Dominie Frelinghuysen, engaged in masked balls and private theatricals. That wise man preached, pleaded, and protested against those departures from Christian propriety in vain. They persisted in spite of him, and made his place so uncomfortable that he finally resigned his pastorate and sailed for Holland. On the passage he disappeared, but whether he fell overboard by accident, or walked over in a moment of insanity, was never known. The good people of his Church believed that he was picked up while floating on the sea, and landed on some unknown remote island, where he lived a hermit's life. For a long time they expected his return, laden with the rich fruits of silent meditation to be distributed for their benefit. But they never saw him again, though they did see the wisdom of his counsels when they beheld the spread of immorality and scandal among their children in consequence of their entering into the amusements, and following the example, of those gay strangers in scarlet coats."

The next morning our lively little party sallied forth to see the many objects of interest to intelligent visitors in this fine old city. Among these was the Schuyler Mansion, especially attractive to the colonel because of the high character, moral and military, of the distinguished patriot soldier who built it, and who for many years dispensed a princely hospitality within its spacious walls.

The colonel spoke with enthusiastic warmth of the generous treatment at this mansion of Burgoyne and his officers after their capture at Saratoga. So courteous and so attentive to their wants was this illustrious soldier that Burgoyne was deeply moved, and said,—

"You show me great kindness though I have done you much injury."

GENERAL SCHUYLER'S MANSION, ALBANY.

"That was the fate of war," replied the generous Schuyler, "let us say no more about it."

Mrs. Schuyler nobly seconded her husband's graceful courtesy, and one evening her distinguished and honored guest was so deeply moved as to say, with tears in his eyes,—

"Indeed, this is too much for the man who has ravaged their lands and burned their dwellings."

The young folks of the party were amused by an anecdote of Schuyler's second son, an arch, active little fellow of seven years, who, one morning, rushed into the saloon occupied by Burgoyne and his suite, and, after shutting himself inside the door, exclaimed,—

" You are all my prisoners ! "

" A boyish freak that," observed the colonel, " but under the circumstances it added not a little to the melancholy of the dejected prisoners of war."

STREET VIEW IN ANCIENT ALBANY.

When, in the course of their walk, they came to the intersection of North Pearl and State streets. the colonel produced a picture of that part of the city as it was three quarters of a century ago.

Pointing to the gable-ended house at the nearer corner, he said,—

"That house was built for a parsonage, of bricks, tiles, iron, and wood-work imported from Holland. It was finished in mahogany and elegantly ornamented with carvings in high relief in 1657. Its last occupant was an eccentric old bachelor, whom the boys regarded as some fierce Bluebeard or ogre. When his tall, thin figure, with its bullet head sprinkled with thin gray hair, appeared on the sidewalk, they fled, fancying he was growling,—

> "'Fee, fo, fum,
> I smell the blood of an Englishman.'

"Though not so terrible as the boys imagined, he was by no means a good citizen."

We have not space to describe more of what our party saw in Albany, but only to say that they spent several very agreeable days there, and then, after visiting Stone Ridge, the Falls of Tivoli, and Greenbush, they turned their steps toward the bustling city of Troy, six miles higher up the river, and one hundred and fifty-one miles from New York.

CHAPTER XIII.

FROM TROY TO THE FALLS OF THE BATTENKILL.

UR party spent a day in Troy, partly for the sake of enjoying the beautiful view from the summit of Mount Ida, which rises abruptly directly

VIEW OF TROY FROM MOUNT IDA.

behind the city, and partly to cross the river to see the United States Arsenal at West Troy. Of the former Clarence remarked,—

216   SUMMER DAYS ON THE HUDSON.

A Roman Catholic college.   Priests and their masters.

"This view is not equal in grandeur to the scenery of the Highlands and the Katzkills, but it is very, very beautiful."

"And the Katzbergs, looming up in the distance, are at least suggestive of the wild grandeur which you miss immediately about you," added Mrs. Stuart.

"What is this huge pile of buildings?" inquired Edith, pointing to a towered edifice which crowns the mount.

"Unfortunately, a Roman Catholic college," replied the colonel, "a school for training priests to hold the consciences of ignorant people in subjection to the rulers of a Church which is corrupt both in doctrine and morals—a Church which wields its spiritual power for political ends, and which is the most dangerous enemy with which our free institutions have to contend."

"You are pretty hard on the Catholics, sir," said Clarence.

"Not on the Catholics, my boy, they are only deceived; but on their *ruling* priests. I say *ruling* priests, because the great body of the Catholic priests are practically slaves to the higher ecclesiastics, whose commands they dare not disobey. Hundreds of them are, no doubt, kept from renouncing their positions by fear of that unsleeping

From Troy to the Falls of the Battenkill. 217

The arsenal at West Troy. What Edith hated. .

vengeance which dogs and ruins an apostate priest in spite of our laws and sympathies."

To these remarks, uttered with deep feeling, no one ventured a reply; and, after rambling to see the view from different points, they retraced their steps to the city below.

The arsenal at West Troy, across the river, with its delightful promenade along the river-bank, its numerous shops, military machines, store-houses, quarters, etc., gave them an agreeable afternoon employment, and afforded them not a little information respecting Uncle Sam's preparations for war in time of peace. As they were leaving, however, Edith excited a general laugh by the warmth with which she exclaimed,—

"Well, I don't care! I'd rather visit one church than thirty arsenals."

"Hoity, toity! Is that the way you estimate your uncle's profession, Miss Edith?" demanded the colonel in a tone of affected anger.

"I can't help it, dear uncle," replied Edith with moistened eyes, "war *is* horrible. I hate it."

The bustle caused by a crowd of people hastening from the ferry-boat prevented any further remark. When the boat put out their attention was taken up by the beauty of the river scene, with its steamboats and sailing craft: the city sitting proudly on

10

Views from Diamond Hill.

RENSSELAER AND SARATOGA RAILROAD BRIDGE.

its right bank, and the long railroad bridge stretching across the stream, looking like a huge cable in
the distance.

From Troy our party ascended the river four
miles, by a hired conveyance, to Lansingburgh.
The drive along the river bank they found to be
most delightful. After a hasty visit to the top of
Diamond Hill, which rises abruptly behind the village, as if in emulation of the Mount Ida of its
Trojan neighbors, they crossed the long bridge which
connects the town with the very attractive village
of Waterford, on the west bank. Their object in

crossing the river at this point was to spend a day
in rambling among the picturesque and grand scenery found about the mouth of the Mohawk. This
fine river, after enriching the fertile country in the
interior of New York through which it flows for
over one hundred and thirty miles, tumbles over a
precipice seventy-eight feet deep, in a stream nine
hundred feet wide, at Cohoes, and then discharges

WATERFORD AND LANSINGBURGH BRIDGE.

its waters into the Hudson a mile below. As our
tourists stood in the garden of the Cataract House
at Cohoes Miss Jennie exclaimed,—

" What a splendid cataract ! "

"It's a miniature Niagara," added Edith.

"It is certainly very beautiful," remarked the colonel. "The Indians must have had a canoe swept over it, for they named it *Ca-hoos*, or a canoe falling, from which word, as I suppose, we get our less euphonious Cohoes."

Anxious to see as much of the Hudson as possible, our travelers drove the next day from Waterford to Stillwater. They found the stream too swift for navigation, but the country was rich and picturesque in its highly cultivated soil, its wooded hills, its flocks and herds, and thrifty-looking homesteads.

"We have had a grand drive," said the colonel, after they had seated themselves in the hotel at Stillwater. "We are now in a region esteemed sacred by every true American, because of the great military events which transpired hereabouts in our Revolutionary war.. We will to-morrow drive over the ground on which our patriot fathers fought and won the battles which ended with the surrender of the British General Burgoyne and his entire army. After Bunker Hill it was their first *grand* success."

We have not space to follow our tourists on their ride the next day over this famous battle ground, nor to repeat in detail the colonel's enthusiastic but truthful story of the campaign which promised so much to the invaders at its opening, but ended so disastrously to their arms. We can only give its substance, and say that in 1777 General Burgoyne, with seven thousand troops and a fine force of artillery, marched from Quebec to Lake Champlain, while Colonel St. Leger advanced with seven hundred troops toward the Mohawk Valley with the intention of occupying Albany. Meanwhile General Clinton was to ascend the Hudson from New York with another army and co-operate with Burgoyne. The plan promised to place our patriot army between three hostile armies, and crush both it and the Revolution by a single blow. But God willed it otherwise. St. Leger was forsaken by his Indian allies, and beaten back from Fort Schuyler. Burgoyne's foraging parties were driven from Vermont, whither they had been sent to secure supplies for his army, by General Stark. Clinton did not make his appearance from below, and the British general was obliged to quit his intrenched camp at Wilbur's Basin, and attack the patriot army in its fortified position. He was resolutely met, and compelled to retire with serious loss. About two weeks after he made a second attempt on the American position, but with no better result. Discouraged and embarrassed, he next determined to retreat to

Fort Edward, but was anticipated by the patriots, who had by this time occupied that post in force. Finally, seeing no way to save his army, either by

BURGOYNE'S ENCAMPMENT AT WILBUR'S BASIN.

retreating or fighting, Burgoyne surrendered his whole command with all its equipments.

"That was a glorious day for our cause!" exclaimed Arthur with enthusiasm.

"Yes, it was," replied the colonel. "The forty brass cannon, the camp equipage, and the nearly eight thousand prisoners we gained, were great prizes to draw in the lottery of the war; but the *prestige* of the victory was vastly more. It encouraged the patriots wonderfully. It also convinced the world that they were in deadly earnest, and that their final triumph was at least a possibility."

"I remember an incident of Burgoyne's last battle," said Clarence, "which deeply impressed me when I read the history of the Revolution."

"What was it?" asked Mrs. Stuart.

SCENE OF BURGOYNE'S SURRENDER.

"It related to General Fraser, who was the hero of the British forces in the field on that memorable day. Dressed in the brilliant uniform of a field officer, and mounted upon a magnificent iron-gray charger, he rode over the field of battle like a paladin of ancient story, inspiring the courage of the troops, and directing their movements with masterly skill. Colonel Morgan, of an American rifle corps, seeing that the issue of the battle depended on the fate of this heroic soldier, called a file of his best marksmen and pointed toward the doomed general, saying :—

"'That gallant officer is General Fraser. I admire and honor him, but it is necessary he should die. Victory for the enemy depends upon him. Take your stations in that clump of bushes and do your duty.'

"In a few seconds the rifle shots of Morgan's men began falling so thickly around the devoted Fraser that one of his aids said :—

"'General, you are a particular mark for the enemy, would it not be prudent for you to retire from this place?'

"'My duty forbids me to fly from danger,' replied the heroic man.

"The next moment a rifle ball laid him low. He was carried from the field to Baron Reidesel's quarters and laid upon a bed. The surgeon examined his wound. 'Tell me,' said Fraser, 'if my wound is mortal. Do not flatter me.'

"There was no hope. The fatal ball had passed through the stomach. The Baroness Reidesel ministered to him with womanly kindness, and heard him exclaim frequently, with sighs :—

From Troy to the Falls of the Battenkill. 225

A general's death.   The good time coming.

"'O fatal ambition! Poor General Burgoyne! O my dear wife!'

"The next morning his mortal career ended. He was buried in the evening, according to his own desire, in a redoubt built on the middle hill of Burgoyne's encampment."

"Shocking!" exclaimed Edith, "and yet he was only one of thousands who were mangled or killed on that fearful day."

"I never hear or read of battles," remarked Mrs. Stuart, "without praying in my heart for the reign of the Prince of Peace—for the day when nations will learn war no more."

"That day is coming, no doubt," replied the colonel. "The details of modern battles, spread before the people as they now are by the newspapers, cause a public dread of war unknown in former times. The common sense of the world, and the higher feeling of humanity created by the loving Gospel of the Lord of life, revolt against it. Courage, Miss Edith! The days of great wars are, no doubt, numbered."

During the drive of thirteen miles from Stillwater to Schuylerville, through a rich plain, to visit the principal scenes of the before-named battles, the young people were quite amused with the old-fashioned rope ferries by means of which the river is crossed in this region. Stopping at Bemis's Heights
10*

they examined one of them closely, and found it to
consist of a big scow pushed by poles reaching to
the bottom of the stream, and kept in its course by

ROPE FERRY.

ropes fore and aft, which were attached by friction
rollers to a stout cable stretched across the river.

"A very ingenious device, that!" exclaimed Arthur, laughing, "but not quite equal to a New York
steam ferry palace."

After spending the night at Schuylerville, our tourists started early the next morning to view the beautiful scenery to be found in its vicinity, as well as to
visit such points of historic interest as the Schuyler

Mansion, and the site of old Fort Saratoga, which in 1745 was the scene of the murder of thirty families by a horde of Frenchmen and Indians, led by a noted partisan named Marin, but spurred on to the dastardly deed of blood by Father Piquet, a crafty Romish priest. The Schuyler Mansion was once the country-seat of General Schuyler, who erected it on the site of one he had previously built, but which was burned by order of Burgoyne—a deed more worthy of an Indian chief than a British officer, and which cost him bitter pangs of useless re-

RAPIDS OF THE FISH CREEK, AT SCHUYLERVILLE.

gret when, after his capture, he learned the nobility of Schuyler's nature.

One of the views which highly gratified our tourists was the cascades of Fish Creek, which is the outlet of the well-known Saratoga Lake.

"It is perfectly beautiful!" exclaimed Jennie, with her usual warmth of feeling. "I love to watch those rapids tumbling beneath the bridge as if they were in a hurry to mix with the noble Hudson."

"This view is indeed picturesque, my dear," replied the colonel, "but it will appear tame to you after you have seen the Falls of *Di-on-on-deh-o-wa*, which we shall visit presently."

"*Di-on-on-deh-o-wa!*" exclaimed Arthur in a sarcastic tone. "If the falls are as singular as their name, they must be very remarkable indeed."

"They *are* remarkable, my boy," replied the colonel, "but the meaning of their Indian name is uncertain."

Returning to their hotel, our party took a carriage and crossed by a bridge, eight hundred feet long, to the east side of the Hudson, for the purpose of enjoying the delightful scenery of the Battenkill valley. Before crossing the bridge, however, they drove to a point up the river from whence they could behold the delightful scene at the confluence of the Battenkill with the Hudson.

"That *is* like fairy-land!" exclaimed Edith. "That

island is lovely. It divides the river, the—what did you call it, uncle?"

"The Battenkill."

"O yes, the Battenkill. The island divides it into

CONFLUENCE OF THE HUDSON AND BATTENKILL.

two channels, and its waters flow into the Hudson without a ripple. It is beautiful—but I don't remember hearing any thing about the Battenkill at school."

"It must have been on your map of the State of New York," rejoined the colonel, "though it is not a large river, only fifty miles from its rise in Vermont to its mouth; but if you have filled your

imaginations with this delicious bit of scenery we
will now drive over the Hudson and ascend the
Battenkill a mile or two."

Two miles from the mouth of this little river they

DI-ON-ON-DEH-O-WA, OR GREAT FALLS OF THE BATTENKILL.

left their carriage in care of the driver, and descended a steep, and somewhat dangerous, precipice on its
south bank to the depth of sixty feet.   There, after
securing good standing places on a shelving rock,

they looked up and gazed with mute astonishment on the roaring stream as it tumbled, in wild confusion, down forty feet into a dark gulf, called by the unattractive name of the Devil's Caldron.

"We have seen nothing equal to this since we were at the Clove in the Katzkills," observed Edith, slightly shivering as she added, "but I don't like the name of this gulf. I think that unpronounceable Indian name you spoke of, uncle, every way preferable."

"Yes, *Di-on-on-deh-o-wa* is more pleasing in *sound* than Devil's Caldron," replied the colonel, "and, as we don't know its meaning, it cannot be as disagreeably suggestive as the other, which represents our conception of every thing that is evil in character, motive, and purpose—but let us clamber back into the light, and trace this fall back through the narrow chasm, which shuts it in for some distance, to where it flows with a more gentle and natural movement."

As you may easily imagine, there was merriment enough to balance the fatigue as they clambered up the precipice, laughing and joking at each other's mishaps. Then, after rambling awhile up the valley, they returned to their carriage, and were driven back to Schuylerville.

The rapids at Fort Miller.

CHAPTER XIV.

FROM THE BATTENKILL TO LAKE GEORGE.

THE next morning our tourists again resumed their drive up the river to Fort Edward. On their way they stopped to take note of the rapids opposite Fort Miller, a fort in the times of the French and Indian wars, but now a thrifty village, fearless of Indian tomahawks, and dreading no greater outward evil than a reverse in the manufacturing world.

As our travelers stood gazing on the foaming waters of the Hudson, dashing with headlong speed down a fall of fifteen or twenty feet in " the course of eighty rods," and over a bed of rough, uneven rocks, ˙Miss Jennie remarked,—

" I should like to see a boat shoot down those rapids ! "

" Not with a human being in it, I hope, Miss Jennie," replied Clarence.

" Why not, sir? " retorted the spirited girl.

" Because he would be sure to lose his life, miss," rejoined Clarence.

" That's not so sure, sir," said Jennie, with an air

of triumph. " Didn't ' Old Put,' as he used to be called, go down these rapids in a boat?"

" He did, my dear," replied the colonel. " But he did it to escape a worse death than drowning. He was out scouting. Having separated from his party, the Indians surprised him alone in his boat, near the eastern shore. He saw that if he tried to row across the stream their rifles would end his life. Then, without hesitation, he boldly pushed his boat into the whirling rapids. Away she flew, leaping over the rocks, spinning round the eddies, dashing through the foam. But Putnam bore a charmed life, and while the Indians stood transfixed with wonder at a deed they dared not imitate, he reached the calm water below in safety. They did not even point a rifle at him, lest they should offend the Great Spirit by whom, as they believed, he was so wonderfully protected. Nevertheless, I question whether Israel Putnam would have ventured the descent except for the purpose of escaping death by savage hands."

" But what one man did another might do, uncle?" said the persistent Jennie.

" He might," rejoined her uncle dryly, "but I should advise him not to try it, unless he was, like Putnam, within the range of an Indian's rifle."

Seven miles more riding, along a charmingly pict-

uresque road, brought them to the village of Fort
Edward, on the east side of the Hudson, where they
proposed to stay until after dinner.

VIEW AT FORT EDWARD.

To obtain a good view of this busy village they
walked to the end of the bridge which connects
Roger's Island with the west shore of the Hudson.
The view they pronounced "delightful." The most
commanding edifice in the village was the colossal
building of the flourishing Seminary of the Methodist Episcopal Church.

They visited the few remains of the fort, which
was of great importance, the colonel told them,

both in the old French and Indian wars and during
the Revolution. A few logs and some traces of
trenches were the only relics to be seen of the scene
of strifes, in which many brave men once measured
their strength in deadly conflict.

While they stood among these relics the colonel
related another instance of Israel Putnam's daring
when the barracks of this fort took fire. Putnam,
hearing the cry of fire, crossed on the ice from
Roger's Island with his men, and took post on a
ladder placed against a building next to the powder
magazine. There he stood, pouring the buckets of
water brought by his men from the river, until the
roof of the building gave way. Even then he would
not give up, but took his stand between the blazing
ruins and the magazine, which a single spark or a
burning cinder might explode in a moment. Amid
showers of sparks the brave man stood, casting the
water, as fast as brought to him, upon the magazine,
until the flames were subdued, and that structure,
with the remainder of the fort, saved. Then the
unconquerable Putnam emerged from the smoke
amid the hurras of his comrades, but with his body
so badly burned that he had to spend a month in
the hospital before he was fit for further duty.

In the afternoon they stopped on their route to
Glen's Falls to visit the grave of the unfortunate

Jenny M'Crea, and also to view the scenery round
Baker's Falls.

These falls they found very imposing.   Here the
river, four hundred feet wide, descends about eighty

BAKER'S FALLS.

feet in the course of a mile, and is broken by the
masses of rocks which impede its course into foaming cascades and rushing torrents.   They spent an
hour or more watching with unabated interest the
restless waters which poured down from above with
unceasing velocity, "an emblem," Mrs. Stuart said,
" of the flow of the eternal years."

In a beautiful cemetery half way between Sandy
Hill and Fort Edward, they stood before a grave at

the head of which they saw a plain marble stone, six feet high, containing the following inscription :—

" Here rest the remains of Jane M'Crea, aged 17, made captive and murdered by a band of Indians, while on a visit to a relative in the neighborhood, A. D. 1777. To commemorate one of the most thrilling incidents in the annals of the American Revolution, to do justice to the fame of the gallant British officer to whom she was affianced, and as a simple tribute to the memory of the departed, this stone is erected by her niece, Sarah Hannah Payne, A.D. 1852."

As our tourists drove through the beautiful village of Sandy Hill toward Glen's Falls, they talked over the sad fate of the beautiful Miss M'Crea, the substance of whose story I will now relate.

Miss Jenny M'Crea was the daughter of a Scotch Presbyterian minister. She was a beautiful, intelligent, graceful girl, so attractive in person and disposition as to be universally beloved wherever known. She was visiting a tory lady in Fort Edward at the time Burgoyne's army approached, where, it seems, she betrothed herself to a young officer in the English army. Influenced, no doubt, by this affection, she refused to accompany her brother, who lived near by, when he fled before the invading army, but remained with her tory friends.

238   SUMMER DAYS ON THE HUDSON.

Jenny M'Crea's tragic death.   A faithful lover.

While Burgoyne was yet at Sandy Hill, a party of savages, seeking captives, for which the English general paid them liberal bounties, suddenly entered the abode of Jenny's friend, and carried off both ladies, intending to take them to the English camp. A negro ran to the fort and alarmed the garrison. A detachment of soldiers was sent after the savages and their fair prisoners. They overtook and fired on them. The Indians were untouched, but one of the musket balls mortally wounded the beautiful Miss M'Crea. The savages, seeing they had lost their prisoner, hastily cut off her scalp, and hastened with it to the camp. The tory friend, who had already arrived, recognized the bleeding scalp by the great length and beauty of the tresses attached to it. Jenny's body was first buried on her brother's farm, was reinterred at Fort Edward, in 1826, with imposing ceremonies, and finally placed in the cemetery where it will repose undisturbed, let us hope, until the morning of the resurrection.

Jenny's lover was so profoundly grieved by the tragic end of his betrothed that he threw up his commission, removed to Canada, and lived a soli-tary single life. Though he lived to be an old man, he never recovered his spirits.

The conversation upon the sad fate of this beauti-ful maiden filled up the time occupied by the drive from Sandy Hill to Glen's Falls. At the former place they noticed the "magnificent sweep" by which the Hudson changes its "course from an easterly to a southerly direction;" at the latter village their attention was engaged by its falls, so admirably described by Hawkeye in Cooper's "Last of the Mohicans." He quaintly says of what he, not unaptly, calls the perversity of the water:—

GLEN'S FALLS.

"It falls by no rule at all. Sometimes it leaps, sometimes it tumbles; there it skips, here it shoots; in one place 'tis white as snow, and in another 'tis green as grass; hereabouts it pitches into deep hol-

lows, that rumble and quake the 'arth, and there-
away it ripples and sings like a brook, fashioning
whirlpools and gullies in the old stone as if 'twere
no harder than trodden clay.   The whole design of
the river seems disconcerted.   First it runs smoothly, as if meaning to go down the descent as things
were ordered; then it angles about and faces the
shores; nor are there places wanting where it looks
backward, as if unwilling to leave the wilderness to
mingle with the salt!"

Our tourists did not find these curious falls quite
up to this quaint yet poetic description, on account
of the comparatively small volume of water then
flowing over them.   They were amused on being
told by a fellow-visitor how the Falls acquired their
present name.   The Indians called them *Che-pon-
tuc*, signifying a difficult place to get round.   The
white settlers named them Wing's Falls, after a soldier named Abraham Wing.   Years after, a son of
this man, while at a convivial party, agreed to trans-
fer his right to name the falls to John Glen, on condition that the latter gentleman would pay for the
supper of the company.   Glen forthwith posted
hand-bills all along the road from the settlement to
Albany announcing the new name, which, being
readily accepted by the people, has designated them
ever since.

"Why, that Wing fellow was a regular Esau!" exclaimed Clarence.

"And threw away his chance of making his name immortal on earth," added Edith.

"I don't think that was a very serious loss," said Arthur. "What good is it to Glen now that his name is attached to these falls? And will not the story of their sale carry Wing's name as far down the stream of time as the waters will carry Glen's? Besides, what does the whole affair show more than that both Wing and Glen were drinking roysterers? Pshaw! I wouldn't give a pebble from the foot of this fall for such immortality!"

The whole party laughed most heartily at Arthur's speech. The colonel responded by saying:—

"Really, my boy, I was not aware that you were so much of a philosopher—but let us away. By driving smartly we may reach Jesup's Falls before sundown."

Pausing on their way to see the great dam and boom which span the Hudson, and hold back the logs sent down from the wilderness, a few miles above Glen's Falls, they pushed on between lofty hills, through scenery which was sometimes picturesque, then rugged and grand, but rarely tame. It was too near dusk when they reached the foot of Jesup's Great Falls to permit them to stop. So

11

they drove on to the village beyond, where they spent the night.

KAH-CHE-BON-COOK, OR JESUP'S GREAT FALLS.

They were now fairly on their way to the wilderness. They had entered the borders of that great Adirondack region, which includes a tract of country equal in size to the State of Connecticut, stretching away from Lakes George and Champlain on the east, to the St. Lawrence on the north and west, and reaching from the Canada line on the north, to Booneville on the south. It is the paradise of sportsmen, and the delight of such tourists as love nature in her own proper guise, and who are willing to dispense with the luxurious elegances of the modern hotel, and put up with plenty, unadorned by the graces of art at such places of entertainment as they may find. Our travelers had made up their minds to endure cheerfully whatever privations they might be called to suffer, as the price of enjoying the wild scenery of the Upper Hudson, and of increasing their strength by inhaling the pure air of the mountain and forest, and by the toil of rough, but not too severe, travel.

Jessup's Great Falls, or *Kah-chc-bon-cook*, as the Indians called them, engaged their attention the next morning. A "grand fall," they pronounced it, truly enough. It extends more than a mile, in the course of which the river descends some one hundred and twenty feet, rushing, in some places, through deep rocky chasms and over lofty precipices.

After viewing these fascinating falls, they drove several miles along the river bank, to a point where the active Sacandaga shakes hands with the Hudson, which, at that point, flows sluggishly along, as if taking rest preparatory to its gigantic leaps at *Kah-chc-bon-cook* below.

As our tourists re-entered their carriage after strolling for an hour round the mouth of the Sacandaga, rain began to fall. Driving as rapidly as was consistent with mercy to their horses, they soon reached a hotel which they found on the banks of the Hudson, at a point where Luzerne Lake tumbles in charming cascades over a steep bluff into the river below. The Indians named this spot *Tia-sa-ron-da*, or, The Meeting of the Waters.

CONFLUENCE OF THE HUDSON AND SACANDAGA.

The rain detained them over that and the ensuing day, which was the Sabbath. But they were in an excellent inn, they wrote up their notes of their journey that afternoon, they heard good, faithful preaching in the village on Sunday, and therefore had no cause to complain or fret. On Monday morning they sallied out, visited the falls, and viewed the high banks at their foot, where, tradition said, an Indian messenger to the English General Burgoyne, when pursued by some patriots, leaped twenty-five feet across and escaped. Then, after

LUZERNE LAKE.

spending a pleasant morning amid the attractive scenery of Luzerne, they departed for Lake George, where they intended to remain a few days, to recruit themselves, before penetrating the depths of the Adirondack wilderness.

CHAPTER XV.

FROM LAKE GEORGE TO THE PEAK OF TAHAWUS.

IN going to Lake George our tourists left the valley of the Hudson at Luzerne, and drove eleven miles through a thickly wooded, picturesque, and partially cultivated country. Their reasons for this were, that the scenery of the valley between Warrensburgh and Luzerne is "not particularly interesting," and that the younger members of the party were desirous of spending a few days at that popular place of resort for summer visitors. In harmony with this part of their plan, they had forwarded the principal part of their baggage from Troy to the care of mine host of that magnificent caravansera, the Fort William Henry Hotel.

Their somewhat fatiguing, but health-giving travel since leaving Troy, had prepared them to enjoy the luxurious living of this fashionable spot, and, for a day or two, they lost somewhat of their enthusiasm for fine scenery, and for ascertaining the historical and traditional incidents associated with particular localities. But their minds were too vigorous and healthy to be long satisfied with the monotony of the lounging, hum-drum life led by most of the visitors. Hence, the young folk, after a few days of idleness, besought the colonel to lead them to the varied points of historic interest in the vicinity.

This he gladly did, for much as he enjoyed fine views, it was the human interests connected with places which most affected him. And after he had recalled the fierce struggles between Huron and Mohawk, Frenchman and Englishman, Tory and Patriot, which had taken place in the not-very-distant past on the shores of this transparent little sheet of water, Arthur only expressed what all the others felt when he said,—

" Lake George seems like another place since you have related these facts, sir."

" Yes," added Edith, " for now when I look out upon the lake I almost expect to see a fleet of Huron canoes, coming to make war on the Mohawks, in the woods behind us."

" And I," said Clarence, " am ever fancying I hear the war-whoop of the Indian or the rattle of musketry."

" Not very charming fancies, I confess," replied the colonel; " nor are they wholly repulsive, if we consider their moral significance. The mutual slaughters among the Indians thinned their numbers, and made it less difficult for civilized men to occupy a country the savages never would have improved. The strifes between the lion flag of England and the lilies of France gave these broad lands to Protestantism; the contests of the redcoats and the patriots helped to make this great continent a broad arena in which freedom might fight its battles, and prove to the nations that vast masses of men can be self-governed—that the ballot is better for all parties than the bayonet."

"I never looked at these old wars in this light before," replied Jennie, with a gravity so unusual for her that it excited a smile, and Clarence laughingly remarked to the colonel,—

"I really think, sir, that Miss Jennie will turn into a philosopher before we get through with our tour."

"There is just as much danger of that as there is of your becoming a *wit*," retorted Jennie with a most withering glance at Clarence.

"You are fairly hit now, Clarence," said Arthur, laughing.

"I acknowledge it," replied the young man; and then looking meaningly at Jennie, he added, "I will let the arrow stay in the wound as young ladies do when wounded with shafts from Cupid's bow."

Jennie blushed and frowned under this scarcely courteous counter-stroke. She was about to reply, when Mrs. Stuart, after shaking her finger at Clarence, asked the colonel,—

"When shall we resume our exploration of the Hudson?"

The colonel named the following Monday, to the satisfaction of all. And when Monday morning arrived they started in high spirits for Warrensburgh, over a plank-road, through a hilly country. Here,

CONFLUENCE OF THE HUDSON AND SCARRON.

at noon, they arrived, often pausing on their way to enjoy what Edith said was "one of the sweetest scenes on the whole river." It was the confluence

11*

A monstrous pile of rocks.

of the Hudson with the Scarron. This river is called Schroon on the maps. This is a corruption of Scarron, the name given to a beautiful lake and river by the French, in honor of the widow of the poet Scarron, but who is better known as Madame de Maintenon.

This scene was in a delightful little valley. The waters met at a lovely spot shaded by elms and other spreading trees, and formed a picture of beauty and repose in strong contrast with the rugged hills around.

"What a monstrous pile of rocks!" exclaimed Arthur, pointing to a craggy elevation on the north side of the valley.

"That is called the Thunder's Nest," replied the colonel, "probably because the Indians, who knew nothing of electricity, supposed that thunder was produced by spirits who haunted lofty isolated spots."

Our tourists were surprised to find Warrensburgh a thrifty leather manufacturing village on the banks of the Scarron, and near the borders of the wilderness. As they had thirty miles to drive before reaching the village of Scarron Lake, where they intended to spend the night, they only stopped long enough to refresh themselves and rest their horses. They found the roads running through a rolling valley in which the scenery was much diversified.

The ride was delightful, though it was rather long, and their team was evidently much fatigued when they arrived, late in the evening, at the village.

At this place another surprise met them in the morning. They found a tasteful mansion, called Isola Bella, built on an island on the lovely Scarron Lake, and occupied by a Colonel Ireland, who traces his ancestry back to one of the bold barons who accompanied William the Conqueror from Normandy to England. They had not expected to find such a scion of the proud old British aristocracy in the wilderness.

Scarron or Schroon Lake delighted them, as also did Paradox Lake, in its neighborhood. Ascending the valley a few miles, they reached Root's Inn that evening, where they found several sportsmen, some of whom were about to enter the wilderness, while others had just returned from it.

Our party was now fairly in the wilderness. Beyond Root's they found the roads rough, the hills steep, the forest vast and solitary, its deep silence only broken by the sighing of the restless wind, or the bubbling of the laughing brook. Here and there they saw the lonely cabin of a settler. At some points the top of a lofty hill afforded a grand view, which amply repaid for the toil of the ascent to it. As they advanced the roads became rougher

and rougher, but the air, every-where pure and redo-
lent of the scent of the pine, the hemlock, and the
balsam, was delicious and invigorating. They enjoyed the drive. Nevertheless they were not sorry
when they reached the Tahawus House, where they
concluded to remain until the next day.

Here they found it necessary to change their
team, and to procure guides who should accompany them in their further explorations. Their next
day's ride was over a corduroy road, that is, a road
built of logs, and a more jolting, jamming ride none
of them, the colonel only excepted, had ever experienced. But, inspired by the invigorating air, and

ADIRONDACK VILLAGE.

accepting their disagreeables with merriment, they
found health, if not absolute enjoyment, in it. Never
perhaps had any of them eaten with richer gusto, or

slept more sweetly, than they did that night at Adirondack village.

This almost forsaken village was made their head-quarters, from whence they proposed to sally forth on foot, and in suitable garments, to visit the most noticeable scenery of this interesting region, which has been very fitly named by its admirers, "The Switzerland of America."

There was no little fun among them when they first met, after dinner, arrayed in their wilderness attire. The gentlemen had on hunting shirts, coarse pantaloons, huge heavy boots, felt hats, and stout buckskin gloves. The ladies, still more metamor-phosed, appeared in short woolen dresses, hoods, and capes, stout boots reaching to the knees, and gloves with gauntlets fastened above the elbows. For a few moments witticisms flew about like leaves in an autumn storm, but in a short time the fitness of their costumes to the work before them was so obvious that they ceased to laugh, and gave them-selves to the task of following their guides.

This task was by no means a light one, for their way, after crossing the Hudson by a rude bridge, led through a tangled growth of wild raspberry bushes, and then up a winding mountain path across which lay many a noble pine, killed by the winter's blast or by the lightning's stroke. Boulders covered with green moss were also sunk in the soil. Over these obstacles they had to climb, and they were not sorry when they reached a lovely little lake to

FIRST BRIDGE OVER THE HUDSON.

hear their guides say they would camp there for the night.

"Camp here!" exclaimed Jennie, with a scornful twist of her rosy lips, "why, where in the world are we to sleep!"

The guides soon answered that question by proceeding to erect a cabin of poles and bark, which they divided, by hanging up a blanket, into two parts, one for the ladies, and the other for the gentlemen. For beds they cut a quantity of hemlock boughs, which the guides laughingly assured the ladies were "a sight easier and sweeter to sleep on than hoss hair or goose feathers."

A delicious supper in the woods.

While one of the guides was giving the finishing strokes to the cabin, the other was off on a rude raft fishing for trout in the lake. On his return with a

BARK CABIN AT CALAMITY POND.

plentiful supply of that delicious fish, supper was prepared upon the clean grass.

"This isn't quite up to the style of the Fort William Henry House, is it, Clarence?" asked Arthur, as he was rubbing the grease from his fingers in the fresh grass.

"Not quite. But you never eat such trout as these anywhere else, eh, Arthur?" responded Clarence, smacking his lips by way of giving epicurean emphasis to his words.

"Nor such slapjacks," added Jennie.

Then a pleasant dispute arose as to whether it was the superior quality of the trout and slapjacks or the sharpness of their appetites which made their supper so relishable. This point was never settled, I believe, because the dispute was broken off by the sad story which led the beautiful lake at their feet to be named " Calamity Pond."

They were told by the guides that about thirty years since, when the iron works at Adirondack village were in operation, Mr. David Henderson, one of the Iron Company, went out on the lake in a scow. In landing he tried to place his pistol on a flat rock near the margin of the lake, holding the muzzle in his hand. By some means it went off, and the ball entered his body, making a mortal wound of which he died in half an hour. His body was sent to his home in Jersey City, N. J., and his friends, at great cost, erected an elegant sandstone monument upon the rock where he perished.

The relation of this story was followed by that of others from their wide-awake guides, respecting adventures both comic and tragic in the forests. These stories occupied their attention very agreeably until the gathering gloom warned them that it was time to seek repose upon their hemlock couches within the cabin. The young ladies protested that " they should not sleep a wink on such a bed," but when they appeared next morning with faces rosy and fresh, Clarence jocosely suggested that "they must have slept without winking."

While their good-natured guides prepared a breakfast of trout, slapjacks, crackers, and coffee, our tourists continued to make their first forest toilet on the shore of the lake. If it was not done as tastefully as in an elegant boudoir, it was certainly performed with more merriment. The young men offered all sorts of inflated compliments to the fair dryads, as they facetiously named their laughing cousins, and were paid in return with mock protests against their attentions, which the young ladies, being "nymphs of the woods," could not condescend to receive from such "uncouth ogres." Thus, if they did not partake of a "feast of reason" before breakfast, they sharpened each other's wits and sat down to their rustic breakfast with flashing eyes and with appetites, as Arthur put it, "sharp as the hooks which had brought the delicious trout to their frying-pan."

Breakfast being over, they resumed their journey toward Mount Tahawus. Their road was nothing but a hunter's trail. It was not easily seen except by the practical eyes of their guides. It was, as Arthur said, "a very hard road to travel." But the pure, bracing air enabled them to laugh at diffi-

culties and to press on. Presently they came to
a pretty little stream, the Opalescent River, at
point where it receives the waters of Lake
Colden, glimpses of
which they caught oc-
casionally through the
trees.

The stream they
found to consist of a
series of rapids and
cascades, here leaping
over huge boulders
weighing a thousand
tons or more, and
there sweeping across
beds of smooth glitter-
ing pebbles of opales-
cent feldspar, of which
the bed of the stream
was full.

"How beautiful!"
exclaimed Mrs. Stu-
art, pointing to a shal-
low spot on which the

FALL IN THE OPALESCENT RIVER.

sun was shining in full splendor. "Mark the rich
colors of those stones; some are deep blue, others
are brilliant green; still others are pearly white. I

From Lake George to the Peak of Tahawus. 259

The Hanging Spear.   At the foot of the mountain.

never saw any thing of the kind so exquisitely beautiful."

In saying this, she only expressed what all the rest felt. By and by they came to a spot where the river fell more than fifty feet between a narrow chasm in the rock into a gloomy basin.

" That is grand ! " exclaimed Arthur.

" It must be a glorious sight when the stream is full," added Clarence.

" The Indians, always poetical in naming natural objects, call this fall *She-gwi-en-dawkwe*, or The Hanging Spear," observed the colonel, " and it does not require a very vivid imagination to perceive the fitness of the name."

Up the valley of the Opalescent our tourists slowly picked their way to the foot of the Peak of Tahawus. It took them over four hours to walk six miles, and then, to refresh themselves, they rested in a bark camp left by some previous tourists. They were now in a wild, solitary spot amid stunted trees, near the lair of the wild cat, and in the vicinity of one of the chief springs from which the mighty Hudson flows.

To climb Mount Tahawus and return to this camp by evening was their task for the afternoon. Their guides told them that few ladies had ever attempted it ; " the few who had did not regret it."

Climbing a pathless mountain.

"Then we will attempt it. What woman has done woman can do again," replied Mrs. Stuart in a mock heroic tone, intended to excite the merry laugh which it caused.

CLIMBING MOUNT TAHAWUS.

To climb two miles over a pathless mountain at an angle of nearly forty-five degrees is, indeed, no light adventure, as our tourists soon found. But they had health, energy, pride of character, and strong wills to sustain them. They pressed on, now winding round a moss-covered boulder, then creeping beneath or pushing between the branches of the dwarf pines and spruces which stood in their path. Here they found an open spot where the wild *oxalis* grew; there they crossed a grove of ancient balsams a hundred years old, but less than five feet high, or walked on a carpet of moss and lichen. At last they rose above the line of the forest, and found themselves on steep rocky slopes and narrow ledges along which they had to creep clinging to the strong mosses or grasping a gnarled shrub, which had its roots in the fissures of the rock. Glad indeed were they when they lighted upon a spring of very cold water which trickled from the mountain's breast, to aid in giving birth to the Hudson. They drank its limpid water and were refreshed. Then on again they pressed, cheered by the shout of a guide who had reached the peak, until they found themselves triumphantly seated on the bare rock which forms the summit of Tahawus, "the Sky Piercer," where they were some six thousand feet above the level of that sea on which they had sailed so pleasantly a few weeks before in the little steam yacht which had carried them to Sandy Hook.

Here they found a hut built of loose stones and covered with moss, the friendly work of some previous tourists. Under the lee of this rude structure they sat down to enjoy the vast landscape spread

out before their wondering eyes.   Near them were
Mounts Colden and M'Intyre.   Beyond these Mounts
Emmons and Seward, Whiteface Mountain, and the

HOSPICE ON THE PEAK OF MOUNT TAHAWUS.

Giant of the Valley.   But over these they looked
far out to the St. Lawrence valley on the north; on
the east they saw the ever charming Green Mountains, and beyond the gray-head of Mount Washington, the king of the White Mountain chain.
Southward rose the mysterious Katzbergs; while on
the west appeared the mountain ranges of Herkimer
and Hamilton Counties, in New York.

They were delighted with the countless variety
of objects embraced in this almost peerless view:
Forests that seemed boundless; small lakes gleam-

ing amid the trees; Lake Champlain, stretching one hundred and forty miles to the eastward, dotted with white sails; and rivers winding like silver threads through their luxuriant valleys.

" I shall never forget this, as long as I live," said Jennie.

" Nor I!" "nor I!" added the others in quick succession.

" It is one of the grandest views in the world," remarked the colonel.

They remained on the Peak of Tahawus, feasting on its scenery and talking of the times of old, when none but Indian savages roamed over the vast spaces at their feet, until the rapidly increasing coolness of the air reminded them that the afternoon was declining, and suggested the propriety of their descent to the forest below. This was accomplished in far less time, and with much less toil, than the ascent. They reached their bark camp at the foot of the mountain in good season, with such an appetite for their simple supper as most of them had never previously possessed. After eating " voraciously," as Edith asserted, they sat round their camp-fire, wondering they felt so little fatigued after such unusual exertion, and listening to stories of war, Indians, and hunters, told by the colonel and the guides, far into the evening.

CHAPTER XVI.

THE next day was the Sabbath, which they spent quietly and thoughtfully in and around their camp, reading their pocket Testaments, listening at intervals to the colonel's observations on certain passages, and attending a morning and evening prayer and singing service, which he conducted. On Monday morning, after partaking of a rude breakfast, heartily enjoyed, they started on their return down the Opalescent Valley to Lake Colden, which lies some three thousand feet above tide water, in a high basin formed by adjacent mountain ranges.

"Whew! what cold water this is!" exclaimed Arthur, withdrawing his hand from the margin of the lake. "I should think the fishes would have but cold comfort here."

'There is no fish in this 'ere lake; nothing but lizards and leeches," remarked one of the guides.

"What, no trout?" asked Jennie, looking quite disappointed at the prospect of eating another forest dinner without trout.

"No, my dear, not a trout swims these cold waters," replied the colonel. "This spot seems conse-

LAKE COLDEN.

crated to the goddess of solitude and silence, for birds are almost as scarce as fish."

After wandering about the shores of this lonely lake at their own sweet will, and regaling themselves on the remains of their supplies, they sauntered slowly back, by way of Calamity Pond, to their head-quarters in Adirondack village.

12

They were fresh enough, after a brief rest, to go out toward evening to see the Iron Dam that Dame Nature, in one of her freaks, had thrown across a stream which is one of the sources of the Hudson. This was nothing less than a massive dyke of iron, stretching across the valley, and barring in the waters like an artificial dam.

" This is wonderful! " exclaimed the colonel. " It seems placed here to attract the eyes of men, and to guide them to the measureless quantities of iron ore which lie hidden in the bowels of these everlasting hills."

They were then informed, by one of their guides, that the mineral riches of these solitary hills were hidden from white men's eyes until about fifty years ago. At that time an Indian hunter appeared one day at some iron works in North Elba. Taking a lump of iron ore from beneath his blanket, he showed it to a Mr. Henderson, saying, with a knowing expression in his eyes,—

" You want to see 'um ore ? Me find plenty—all same."

" Where did it come from ?" asked Henderson, with an assumed air of indifference.

Pointing to the south-west the Indian replied, " Me hunt beaver all 'lone, and find 'um where water run over iron dam."

Prompted partly by curiosity and partly by the hope of gain, Henderson organized an exploring party, followed the Indian, found the Iron Dam,

THE IRON DAM.

discovered that boundless quantities of valuable ore lay waiting the skill of man, procured partners, purchased the lands, and established iron works at an outlay of hundreds of thousands of dollars. The enterprise, successful at first, failed in 1856, owing partly to a fearful flood which devastated many of the works, and partly to the depressed condition of the iron trade. Henceforth the village was deserted of its inhabitants.

Their next day's journey was in a stout, springless wagon, over a merciless corduroy road, twenty-six weary miles, to Pendleton.

"We have had a pretty tough ride to-day," said Clarence, after stretching his sore and stiffened limbs on a grass plot in front of the house which was to be their home for a day or two.

"It was rather jolty," replied Arthur, "but I think the view we had of that sweet patch of fairy-land they call Sandford Lake was at least part payment for the shaking we got."

The party agreed to this opinion, as they did also to the colonel's proposal of an idle evening and an early hour for retirement.

But fatigue in that pure air soon wore off, and the next morning found them all cheerful, and eager to start in boats for Harris's Lake.

Boating on the lake was a new and pleasant experience to our tourists; "Infinitely easier than roughing it on corduroy roads," Arthur asserted, in a tone made emphatic by the twinges of his still aching bones. The lake they found to be a beautiful sheet of water: the rapids at its head Mrs. Stuart pronounced "very picturesque indeed," set

off, as it was, by the rounded form of Goodenow
Mountain in the distant background. The aspects
of Mount Tahawus, (Mount Marcy,) Mount Colden,

RAPIDS AT THE HEAD OF HARRIS'S LAKE.

and Mount M'Intyre, seen from a point of view
below the rapids, Clarence declared to be "grand,
even if they are old friends," an opinion from which
no one felt disposed to dissent.

Early next morning they launched their boats on
the placid face of Rich's Lake, a miniature body of
water only two miles and a half long, but surrounded by many peculiar objects. One of these was the
Goodenow Mountain, rising from its southern shore
to the height of more than fourteen hundred feet,
and crowned with a curiously formed "rocky knob:"

the other was a wood-crowned limestone penin-
sula, called Elephant Island.

"See!" exclaimed Arthur, pointing to a protrud-
ing rock, at the corner of the promontory, "that
looks for all the world like an elephant standing in
a stall."

"You are not the first to perceive such a like-
ness," replied the colonel; "that, with other singular

ELEPHANT ISLAND.

resemblances to that animal to be seen in these
rocks, gave this little islet its name."

"But is it really an island?" asked Edith. "It
looks as if it jutted out from the shore."

"So it does, my dear," replied the colonel. "But

when the lake is full the waters flow over the short neck of land which joins it to the main, and make it an island."

Passing out of this pretty lake, they soon reached the confluence of the Hudson and Fishing Brook. Here they left the boats, and walked half a mile through the forest to see a clearing and a saw-mill, said to be the first on the Hudson.

The saw-mill stood at the head of a wild gorge, through which the water ran with picturesque wildness from the pond above.

The *clearing* was a great novelty to all but the colonel. They had never before seen the face of a patch of forest when undergoing man's first efforts to subdue it from its wilderness condition. As they were looking at the field, almost covered with stones and charred stumps, Arthur said,—

"It doesn't seem possible that this piece of land can ever be made into a smooth, highly cultivated field. How can men ever plow between these stumps and boulders?"

"The owner will be likely to put in his first crop without plowing," replied the colonel. "He will loosen its surface with the hoe, and, after dropping his seed, will cover it with the same instrument. The rich, virgin soil will give him a good crop. After taking it off, he will gather the stones into

FIRST SAW-MILL ON THE HUDSON.

heaps. If able, he will pull many of these stumps with a machine worked by oxen; others of them he will reduce to ashes by fire. Then he will put in his plow. It will be slow, rough work the first time:

but year by year it will become easier, and in far fewer seasons than you can readily imagine he will have this field almost as clean and smooth as the surface of a Connecticut meadow."

Returning to their boats, our tourists proceeded by a "carry"—that is, by walking, the guides carrying their baggage and boats—from the junction of the Hudson and Fishing Brook to Lilypad Pond. The distance was only three quarters of a mile, and the walk was an agreeable diversion, albeit the path

FIRST CLEARING ON THE HUDSON.

was none of the smoothest. Another sail, through this pond and Narrow Lake, and then a short walk
12*

over rough boulders, brought them to the outlet of
the beautiful Catlin Lake.

"This is another scene from fairy-land," said

CATLIN LAKE.

Edith, as the light boat sped like an arrow along
the unruffled surface of the water. "I can scarcely
believe that such a charming spot belongs to this
solitude. The fair naiads of these forests must
have conjured it up for our entertainment, and
when we are gone it will dissolve, like a work of
enchantment."

"A very poetical fancy, Edith, and very complimentary to us," replied the colonel, laughing;

Beginning a hard day's journey.

" but, unfortunately for your theory, every summer visitor to these regions finds it just as you see it."

" It is lucky for us that it is so," added Clarence.

" Why so, sir?" asked Edith.

" Because, if the scene were an illusion, and it should happen to dissolve just now, we might find ourselves carried with it into some fairy grotto beneath the lake, which might be more airy and fantastic than would suit our earthly, matter-of-fact natures."

As Clarence made this remark their boat touched the shore. They landed, and found the guides of the other boats, which had preceded theirs, busily preparing a camp for their night's abode.

Their next day's journey put their powers of endurance to a pretty severe test. Not at its beginning, however, for that was a decidedly easy and delightful boat-ride, through a miniature body of water with shores that charmed their eyes with beauty, and which emptied into Catlin Lake through a stony channel.

" This is Fountain Lake," said the colonel, as they stood at the head of its outlet, waiting for the guides to launch the boats. The " carry " of a mile had enabled them " to stretch their legs," as Arthur inelegantly expressed it.

" Why is it called Fountain Lake, sir?" inquired the properly inquisitive Clarence.

" Because it is the first basin which collects water from the springs which give origin to the western branch of our noble Hudson. We shall presently drink from the principal of those springs—that is," the colonel added after a significant pause, " if we have pluck enough to go through the swamp beyond which it lies."

The young men boldly affirmed that they " could stand swamp travel or any thing else. The last week had made them tough as hunters." In the same spirit the ladies declared they had become daughters of the forest, and " could go through the woods as readily as Diana of the ancients."

This merry boasting soon met its test, for, having glided across the two miles' length of Fountain Lake, and ascended Spring Brook as far as their boats could float, they entered the swamp. To relieve the guides, who had to carry the boats, each of our tourists carried a small portion of their baggage. With full hands, light hearts, and loud merriment, they plunged into the swamp.

But walking over ground full of holes, stones, and gnarled roots, covered with tangled vines and straggling shrubs, with fallen trees lying every-where across the track, is no laughing matter. Hence, in a short time their jokes died away. They plunged on in silence, broken only by such exclamations as, " O!" " This *is* tough!" " Dear me, how hot it

SWAMP TRAVEL.

is!" " Plague on these monstrous mosquitoes! they are eating me up," etc. Every few moments saw them panting and resting against a prostrate tree, diligently wiping away the perspiration, or peering through the woods with glances which

278   SUMMER DAYS ON THE HUDSON.

Half a mile an hour.   A feast of raspberries.

seemed to say, " O, that we were at the end of the
swamp!"

But all things, swamps not excepted, have an
end, and after an hour's toil they found themselves
half a mile from their starting-point, on more prac-
ticable ground.

" Half a mile an hour!" exclaimed Arthur, puffing vigorously. " I call that lightning express
speed. There is not a steam-engine in the country
that could begin to come up with it. In fact, I'll
back this party against the best locomotive ever
built."

" You mean on *this ground*," added Clarence.

" Faugh!" exclaimed Jennie, laughing scornfully.
" A steam-engine couldn't budge here."

" Come and taste these raspberries!" cried the
colonel, who had moved off into a sort of cut which
had once been made for a canal, intended to unite
the waters of Long Lake with those of Fountain
Lake, but which had never been finished.

The colonel's call attracted them. The ripe raspberries were abundant and refreshing. Their merriment returned, and, after traversing the cut with
comparative ease for half a mile, they found themselves standing at a spring, five feet in diameter,
named Hendrick, in honor of that glorious old navi-
gator, Hendrick Hudson. They were gazing on a

spring which is the fruitful parent of the western branch of one of the finest rivers in America.

" What deliciously cold water!" exclaimed Arthur, after drinking from the shallow pool.

" See those lovely ferns!" cried Edith, pointing to the delicate fronds which adorned the margin of the spring.

After resting awhile in this lovely nook, our tourists resumed their tedious journey through the swamp. They bore it well, but their cheerfulness grew smaller by degrees, until, reaching the end of that fatiguing " carry," they came to Long Lake, on which they embarked, and sailed until they reached a spot near to a sort of forest inn, at which they spent the night.

Long Lake was called *Inca-pa-chow*, or the Linden Sea, by the Indians, because of the numerous Linden-trees growing round its shores. It is thirteen miles long, dotted here and there with lovely islets, surrounded with trees, which grow in some places on points which jut out into its transparent waters, while grand mountains rise loftily in the distance, lending their simple grandeur to the scene.

This lake, they were told, though less than half a mile from Hendrick Spring, the western birthplace of the Hudson, and on the same level, flows into the St. Lawrence, and empties into the Atlantic a

thousand miles north-east of the mouth of the
Hudson.

From Long Lake, where they rested over Satur-

RAQUETTE RIVER.

day and Sunday, our party proceeded to the Raquette River, which flows through it, "like the
Rhone at Geneva." They were astonished at its
size, and at the beauty of its park-like shores.

" Raquette ! Why is it called Raquette River ? " asked Clarence.

" This is a region formerly abounding in moose, and on these shores the Indians once gathered in large numbers to hunt. They came on snow-shoes. Raquette is French for snow-shoe, and hence came the name of the river. There is another opinion, however, which asserts that the Indians named it *Ni-ha-na-wa-te*, Noisy River. But as the stream is no more noisy than its neighbor, the Grass River,

TENANTS OF UPPER HUDSON FORESTS.

this source of the name is rejected by so good a critic in these matters as Lossing."

" I once saw a *moose* in a menagerie," said Edith. " Is it found in these woods now ? "

"Not in droves, my dear," replied the colonel, "but only in small numbers. The white hunter has thinned out the race, as he has also that of the deer, the bear, the otter, and the beaver. The wolf and the panther he has almost blotted from existence, as he will all the others in a few brief years, unless, moved by his interests, he should protect the noble deer. But I doubt not that he and the speculator in lumber, whose short-sighted greed is fast destroying our noble forests, will, in a few years, kill the last of the beasts which have for ages found a home in these grand old woods."

From Raquette River our travelers proceeded by Stony Brook to Spectacle Ponds; and thence, through these three beautiful sheets of water, and a short "carry," to the shores of the upper Saranac Lake, near which they found entertainment at the log-house of a hunter, which was a fair specimen of the homes that the first settlers were in the habit of building before the now almost universal saw-mill enabled them to build "frame" houses.

"There isn't much comfort in a log-house," observed Jennie, with a slight curl of her lip, on the morning of their departure for a trip across the three Saranac Lakes.

"Not much to invite an elegant lounger, whose ideas of comfort were formed in a sumptuous home,

I confess," replied the colonel. "Nevertheless, a
log-house is often the abode of more contentment
and real happiness than are to be found in royal

A LOG-HOUSE IN THE FOREST.

palaces and magnificent mansions. I recollect a
family in Canada, with whom I once found pleasant
entertainment. They were then living in a large
frame house, finely situated on the banks of a lovely little lake. Their farm was large, highly cultivated, very productive, and largely stocked with
superior cattle, sheep, and horses. Their home
was comfortably, not to say richly, furnished. Six
daughters and three sons, all in fine health and
possessing excellent characters, made that house

A finer home but less happiness.

cheerful, and contributed to the happiness of the
father and mother.   One day, while talking with
this stout old farmer, he told me that he married
young, and moved with his bride into what was
then a wilderness.   'Our whole fortune,' said he,
'consisted of an ax, a spade, a hoe, a cow, and a
few trifles which we brought on the creature's back.
We camped out until I built that log-house which
you see on the edge of the barn-yard yonder, and
I tell you, sir, that my wife and I often remark that
our happiest days were spent under its rude, un-
ceiled roof.   We were poor, we worked hard, but
the bird of hope sung its sweet songs in our hearts,
and we enjoyed life amazingly—better, sir, than we
do now in our big house.   I do not mean to say
we are not happy now, sir, but we have so many
cares, and so much to vex us, that we often sigh
for the good old days spent in that dear old log-
shanty.' "

"I guess there was some romance in all that,
uncle," rejoined Jennie.

"Perhaps so, perhaps so," said the colonel, "but
I would have you remember, my dear, that happiness is not the product of either stately or log
walls, of cheap or costly furniture, but of the human
hearts which dwell within the building.   If they are
at peace with God and man their external surround-

ings are of far less consequence than men generally imagine."

Their embarkation on the Upper Saranac Lake put an end to what Jennie, in a whisper to Edith, somewhat disrespectfully called "uncle's preaching." The thirteen miles' trip on this "dark, wild sheet of water" was followed by a short "carry," which led to Round Lake, as the middle Saranac Lake is called, over which they sailed nearly four miles. Thence by a narrow winding stream, beautifully fringed with rushes, lilies, and other plants, they made their way to the Lower Saranac. A delightful sail of six miles on that placid sheet of water, among numerous lovely little islets, brought them by evening to a comfortable forest inn. Here they doffed their rough wilderness garb and resumed their usual dresses. Their journeys by boat and on foot in the wild woods were over. The next day comfortable wagons, drawn by stout horses, bore them rapidly through the Great Au Sable Valley. The magnificence of the scenery afforded them much pleasure. Nevertheless, they were far from displeased on arriving at Port Kent, in the evening, to find that they were about to return to their wonted way of life, amid those comforts of our high civilization to which long habit had accustomed them.

The next day found them on Lake Champlain on their way to Whitehall, whence, by rail and steamboat, they were soon borne back to their point of departure—the Mountain House on Englewood Cliffs—which was their favorite summer resort. When seated on its broad piazza the morning after their return, discussing their tour, the colonel observed :—

" I think we have all richly enjoyed our trip. We have certainly added to our strength and healthfulness. What we have seen of this truly grand river and its adjacent scenery has widened the circle of our knowledge, quickened our powers of observation, and improved our taste for the beautiful in nature. Our conversations respecting the associations, legendary and historical, connected with the localities we have visited have given us a firmer hold of facts we knew before, and have also added somewhat to our mental stores. Altogether, I think our tour may be pronounced sensible, profitable, and exceedingly pleasant."

To this conclusion the whole party gave cordial assent ; Miss Jennie, however, laughingly saying,—

" There is but one drawback to it all—the trip has spoiled our complexions. We are all as brown as gipsies ! "

" I had scarcely noticed that unquestionable fact,"

replied Arthur, and then, lowering his voice, he added, in a tone meant only to reach Miss Jennie's ears, " but the increased brilliancy of your eyes has so lighted up your face that one doesn't observe its deepened color much."

Miss Jennie blushed at this compliment, which, though spoken softly, had caught the colonel's ear. Playfully shaking his finger at Arthur, he said in a significant tone,—

" Arthur, my boy, the words of a flatterer are the seeds of foolish actions, and nothing can give real beauty to the human face but the honor, innocence, and integrity of the soul which dwells behind it."

This gentle rebuke made the color rise in the young man's face. He bowed somewhat awkwardly, but made no reply. Mrs. Stuart, however, came to his relief, saying in her own gentle, playful manner,—

" Let us have peace, my brother. Arthur's pretty words were but as flecks of idle foam, which disappear in a moment. Jennie understood them thus. I trust them both, as I do Miss Edith and Master Clarence. They possess common sense. They respect themselves and us. They will not act imprudently. Let us rejoice, therefore, with unmixed joy, over these happy days spent on our noblest of rivers, trusting that when the stream of time has borne us a little nearer to the great Hereafter, the wishes of our hearts, and theirs also, will be gratified."

The colonel smiled benignly on his sister as he replied:—

"Yes, yes, it is well to be hopeful, but I want these young folks to bear in mind that much, very much of their future will be what they choose to make it. Right aims, pure motives, diligent self-culture, patient waiting on Divine Providence, and supreme loyalty to our loving Redeemer, will make their future life-journey happy, and cause its ending to be but as the beginning of bliss.

The lunch bell put an end to further conversation, as it must also be permitted to do to our story of "Summer Days on the Hudson."